Go For It!

Seriously Cool Puffin Stories

PUFFIN BOOKS

PUFFIN BOOKS

Published by the Penguin Group
Penguin Books Ltd, 27 Wrights Lane, London W8 5TZ, England
Penguin Putnam Inc., 375 Hudson Street, New York, New York 10014, USA
Penguin Books Australia Ltd, Ringwood, Victoria, Australia
Penguin Books Canada Ltd, 10 Alcorn Avenue, Toronto, Ontario, Canada M4V 3B2
Penguin Books (NZ) Ltd, Private Bag 102902, NSMC, Auckland, New Zealand

On the World Wide Web at: www.penguin.com

Penguin Books Ltd, Registered Offices: Harmondsworth, Middlesex, England

First published 2000
1 3 5 7 9 10 8 6 4 2

Set in Baskerville

Made and printed in England by Clays Ltd, St Ives plc

British Library Cataloguing in Publication Data
A CIP catalogue record for this book is available from the British Library

ISBN 0-141-30834-6

Contents

Philip Ridley

The Hooligan's Shampoo

1

What a blue sky! thought Dillon. Not a cloud in sight. And the sea! Smooth as a mirror. My little boat's hardly rocking –

Look! Something's floating towards me! It's very colourful. Looks like one of those bags you get from a supermarket – No! It's a jellyfish! How wonderful! It's sinking now. Lower and lower . . .

The water's so clear. I can see right to the bottom. Look! An octopus! And a whale with a baby whale. And there! A dolphin! Oh, how beautiful –

It's swimming up to me! Higher and higher! Now it's splashing and squeaking beside the boat. What's it trying to say? Splash, squeak, splash, splash –

I know! It wants me to ride on its back.

Yes, Mr Dolphin! Yes! Yes!

I'm climbing over the side of the boat now.

The dolphin is keeping as still as possible for me. Careful! Its back is very slippery. Oh, I'm so excited! I'm going to ride through the ocean on –

'DILLON!'

Darn it! What's Grandpa doing awake? He should be taking his afternoon nap. Ignore him! Nothing must get in the way of –

'DILLON!'

Grandpa's shouting is ruining my daydream. Look! The sky is turning back into my bedroom ceiling –

'DILLON!'

The sea is a blue carpet!

'DILLON!'

The boat is my bed!

'DILLON!'

And the dolphin – oh, beautiful Mr Dolphin – is nothing but a pillow!

'DILL –'

'ALL RIGHT, GRANDPA!' Dillon called. 'I'LL BE RIGHT WITH YOU!'

2

'What took you so long, Dillon? I've been yelling and yelling! My throat feels like sandpaper!'

'Sorry, Grandp –'

'Don't apologize, Dillon. After all, what am I? Nothing but a bedridden old man with hairs on his nose, warts on his chin, and wrinkled from tip to toe. Oh, look at you, Dillon! Hair tangled! T-shirt creased! Jeans crumpled! You've been daydreaming again, haven't you?'

'No, Grandp -'

'Don't deny it, worthless daydreamer! I know you

inside out! Your skull's full of all manner of naughty things, that's why I've got to keep you busy. Now look out of the window and tell me what you see. Strange noises disturbed my nap. What are they?'

'Let's take a look, Grandpa – Aha! Mmm! Ooooo – there's a lorry outside the house opposite. The house that's been empty for so long . . . annnd . . . ooooo! Yes! New people must be moving in, Grandpa!'

'New people! Ugh! Spare me new people! What do they look like, Dillon?'

'I can't see anyone at the moment, Grandpa – Aha! Wait! Mmm – there's a girl!'

'A girl! It's getting worse! Describe her.'

'Ooooo. . . she's got long blonde hair.'

'Ugh!'

'And she's wearing a frilly white dress.'

'Ugh! Ugh!'

'And she's very pretty.'

'Ugh! Ugh! Ugh! Sounds like a hooligan to me!'

'Oh surely not, Grandpa –'

'That's it! Argue with me! Honestly, Dillon, sometimes you're as irritating as an earwig in my underpants! Do something useful and go to the corner shop! I feel a yearning coming on! I need a tangerine to soothe my sore throat. And Dillon . . .'

'Yes, Grandpa?'

'Don't talk to that Hooligan!'

3

Tring! went the bell above the shop door.

'Well, a hungry hello to you, Dillon,' said the shopkeeper.

'And a hungry hello to you, Mr Shopkeeper,' said Dillon.

'What can I get you today? Something for your grandpa no doubt. Well, my shop has something to satisfy every possible yearning. Perhaps a hairy coconut kissed by the tropical sun? Or fine tea from China, scented with bergamot? Or a jar of roasted peppers in olive oil? And here! Something most exotic! Delicious chocolates! Can you guess what's in them –?'

'I've no idea,' interrupted Dillon. 'All I want is a tangerine.'

'A tangerine!' The shopkeeper looked horrified. 'When I have shelves full of tantalizing tinned goods to tap-dance on your taste-buds!'

'Afraid so.'

The shopkeeper sighed and shook his head despondently. 'Over there! In that box!'

Dillon went to the box and saw a solitary tangerine with a maggot, big as a finger, poking out of it.

'I can't buy this!' Dillon declared. 'It's rotten!'

'Rotten indeed!' gasped the shopkeeper. 'I'll have you know that in some far-flung places a maggot is considered a delicacy.'

'Well, you should sell it in far-flung places,' said Dillon, walking towards the door. 'Not here!'

'It'll put hairs on your grandpa's nose!'

'He's got hairs on his nose already. A hungry goodbye to you, Mr Shopkeeper.'

Tring!

4

Grandpa's going to be really annoyed! thought Dillon. I bet he says, 'I could have trained a monkey to get me a tangerine –'

'Watch where you're going please,' said a voice.

Dillon looked up and saw –

'The Hooligan!' he gasped out loud.

'The what?'

'Oh . . . aha . . . mmm, yes! I'm sorry!' stammered Dillon. 'I didn't mean to be rude. It's just that . . . well, that's what my grandpa called you.'

'The Hooligan?' the girl said, smiling thoughtfully. 'Well, please thank your grandpa. I like the name. Although, to be honest, you're a bit of a Hooligan too. You nearly knocked me over, storming down the street like that.'

'Ooooo . . . sorry.'

'Apology accepted.' The girl's smile grew wider. 'I'm going to the shop. Do you want to come with me? Perhaps we can be friends.' She held out her hand.

Dillon flinched away. 'I can't! *We* can't! Grandpa told me not to talk to you.' He started backing down the street. 'And don't buy the tangerine. It's got a maggot in it!'

'Sounds delicious!' said the Hooligan.

5

'I could have trained a monkey to get me a tangerine!'

'But, Grandp –'

'Oh, don't explain! After all, what am I? Just a tangerineless, bedridden old man with hairs on his nose, warts on his chin, and wrinkled from tip to toe. Honestly, Dillon, you're about as much use as a cockroach in my cocoa! You're not going to cry, are you?'

'No, Grandpa –'

'Don't lie, worthless daydreamer! There's tears in your eyes! Get out before they dribble all over the place. The damp will aggravate my rheumatism.'

'But –'

'Go!'

6

Dillon was sitting on his doorstep, drying his eyes, when the Hooligan walked up.

'That Mr Shopkeeper has the strangest things,' she said. 'I didn't even know you could buy locusts dipped in chocolate. You been crying?'

'A little.'

'Why?'

'It's my grandpa. He's always saying nasty things to me! He thinks I'm nothing but a worthless daydreamer.'

'Daydreamer, eh? And what do you daydream about exactly?'

'Ooooo . . . lots of things.'

'Such as?'

'Dolphins.'

'Dolphins!' exclaimed the Hooligan. 'Oh, perr-leeze! How boring! All that squeaking and splashing. What tedious animals!'

'I don't find them tedious at all,' insisted Dillon. 'I find them . . . thrilling!'

'Thrilling! Oh, give me a break. You don't know what thrilling is till you've seen what I've got.'

'G-got? Wh-where?'

'In my room.

'Wh-what is it?'

'A creature. It lives in a large fish tank. Got sharp teeth so it can eat things like this!' She held a hamburger in the air. 'Raw meat! Fresh from the corner shop! And, when my creature eats, there's so much chomping and splashing and gurgling that I go, "Eeeee!" Come and watch! I bet you'll go "Eeeee!" too.'

'Ooooo . . . I'd love to! Really! But . . . mmm . . . well, my grandpa won't let me.'

The Hooligan stared at Dillon for a while, then said, 'Wait here!' She rushed into her house.

When she returned a few minutes later, she was holding a small silver watering-can. 'A present,' she said. 'To cheer you up.'

'Ooooo . . . thank you,' said Dillon, taking the can.

'But . . . what would I want it for?'

'Who knows?' the Hooligan said, dashing back home. 'All manner of things might need watering one day.'

7

That night Dillon lay in bed and looked at the watering-can on his bedside cabinet.

Moonlight glinted off its silver surface. My first gift! thought Dillon. How good of Hooligan to give it to me! I wish I could be her friend. It would be nice to watch her creature eat hamburgers.

And it would be even nicer to . . . hold her hand.

8

What a blue sky! thought Dillon. Not a cloud in sight. And the sea! Smooth as a mirror. My little boat is hardly rocking –

Look! Something's floating towards me! Looks like a tin bath-tub – No! It's a turtle! Oh, how beautiful –

Now it's blowing bubbles beside the boat. What's it trying to tell me? Bubble, bubble –

I know! It wants me to ride on its back.

Yes, Mr Turtle! Yes! Yes!

I'm climbing over the side of the boat now.

The turtle is keeping as still as possible for me. Careful! Its shell is slippery with seaweed. Oh, I'm so excited! I'm going to ride through the ocean on –

'DILLON!'

Darn it!

9

'What a mess you look, Dillon! Have you been daydreaming again?'

'No, Grandp –'

'That's it! Lie to me! After all, what am I? Just a bedridden old man with hairs on his nose, warts on his chin, and wrinkled from tip to toe. Look out of the window! I can smell something very strange. It's tickling my nose hairs – TISHOO!'

'Let me see, Grandpa – Aha! Mmm! Ooooo – Hooligan is washing her hair. I can see her through the bathroom window. There's soapsuds all over the place. Ooooo . . . so many. They're floating out of the window and down the street. Oh, they're . . . remarkable –'

'Don't say "remarkable", Dillon. I've told you before: there's nothing left remarkable in the world. And the least remarkable thing in this unremarkable world is you – TISHOO!'

'Bless you, Grandp –'

'Don't bless me, Dillon! Just go to the shop and get me some milk. What with my sore throat and all this sneezing, I've got a cold coming on. A cup of warm milk might help – TISHOO!'

10

Tring!

'Well, a hungry hello to you, Dillon.'

'A hungry hello to you, Mr Shopkeeper.'

'And what has your grandpa a yearning for today? Perhaps some bamboo shoots with water chestnuts, flavoured with aromatic Madras? Or saffron rice with –?'

'Just milk,' interrupted Dillon.

The shopkeeper shook his head. 'I'm wasted in this place,' he sighed. Then indicated a crate in the corner. 'Over there!'

There was only one bottle of milk left and, when Dillon took it from the crate, he saw –

'It's curdled! Grandpa can't drink this!'

'Course he can,' the shopkeeper insisted. 'In some parts of the world milk is only worth drinking when it's tinged with green. Besides, it'll put warts on your grandpa's chin.'

'He's got warts on his chin already.'

'But –'

Tring!

11

Grandpa's going to be even more annoyed now! thought Dillon. I bet he says, 'You haven't got the sense God gave lettuce –'

'Watch it!'

Dillon looked up and saw –

'Hooligan! Ooooo . . . I'm sorry. Did I nearly walk into you again?'

'You most certainly did,' said the Hooligan. 'But don't worry. I'm getting used to it.' She smiled and fluttered her eyelashes. 'I'm getting another hamburger. Want to come with me?'

'I'd like to but . . . ooooo –'

'Oh, that's right! Your grandpa! I forgot! I must say your grandpa sounds as tedious as your dolphins –'

'I like turtles too!'

'Turtles! Oh, perr-leeze! They're even worse. Nothing but a shell with a head so small it's hardly worth having! Might as well daydream about dustbin lids.' She started walking towards the shop.

'Don't buy the milk,' Dillon called after her. 'It's sour and clotted!'

'Sounds scrumptious!'

12

'You haven't got the sense God gave lettuce!'

'But, Grandp –'

'Oh, don't explain! After all, what am I but a tangerineless, milkless, bedridden old man. You're not crying again, are you?'

'No, Grandp –'

'Liar! Look at those tears! Damp is the last thing my cold needs. Just like you! No consideration – TISHOO!'

'Bless you.'

'Get out!'

13

As Dillon sat on the doorstep drying his eyes, he heard strange noises coming from the Hooligan's house –

Chomp! Chomp!

Splash! Splash!

Gurgle! Gurgle!

'Eeeeeeeeee!'

Hooligan's feeding her creature! he thought. If only I could see it! I bet its sharp teeth make mincemeat of that hamburger –

'Oh, perr-leeze! Do stop crying.'

'Ooooo . . . hello, Hooligan! I didn't hear you walk up.'

'No wonder! You were too busy snivelling!'

'Don't be nasty.'

'I'm being honest, not nasty! And just to prove it – here! Another present for you.'

'Wh-what is it?'

'A bag of earth!'

'A bag of earth! But what would I want a bag of earth for?'

'Who knows?' said the Hooligan, plopping the bag in Dillon's lap. 'All manner of things might need planting one day.'

'TISHOO!'

'Oh, perr-leeze!' gasped the Hooligan. 'What a deafening sneeze!'

'It's Grandpa! He says your shampoo irritates his nose hairs! But . . . well, I think your hair smells lovely.'

The Hooligan smiled and walked back home.

'Thank you for the earth,' Dillon called after her.

14

That night Dillon lay in bed and looked at the bag of earth on his bedside cabinet.

My second gift! he thought. How good of Hooligan to –

'Zzzzz.'

Oh, Grandpa's snoring is disturbing me. I want to think of Hooligan! Not listen to him!

'Zzzzz.'

The way she says 'Perr-leeze'.

'Zzzzz.'

The smell of her hair.

'Zzzzz.'

Holding her hand . . .

15

WHAT a blue sky! thought Dillon. Not a cloud in sight! And the sea! Smooth as a mirror. My little boat is –

'TISHOO!'

– hardly rocking.

'TISHOO!'

Darn it! Grandpa's sneezing will wake him up. Then he'll –

'DILLON!'

Knew it!

16

'Look how ill I am, Dillon! Sore throat! Sneezing! And now I'm shivering so much my dentures are rattling. But are you bothered? No! You're in your room daydreaming!'

'I'm not, Grandp –'

'Don't deny it! Just buy me a blanket. I have a yearning to keep warm.'

17

Tring!

'Well, a hungry –'

'A blanket.'

'My! You're in a bad mood! Why don't you buy some of these delicious chocolates. Have you guessed what's in them yet –'

'I don't care! Just give me a blanket.'

'The chocolates are easier to swallow.'

'Spare me the jokes.'

The shopkeeper sighed and pointed to a shelf. 'Over there! One left, I think.'

'Thank you! Oh, look at the state of it! Full of holes.'

'You're exaggerating, surely!'

'No, I'm not! In fact, it's more holes with a blanket

than a blanket with holes. I can't buy this!'

'But –'

'Chew a locust!'

Tring!

18

Grandpa's going to be more annoyed than ever now! thought Dillon. I bet he says 'You're two tokens short of a toaster –'

'Watch it! You nearly walked into me again –'

'Then *you* watch where *you're* going, Hooligan!'

'My! Who rattled *your* cage?'

'Everyone!'

'Why don't you come with me to buy a –'

'Hamburger! For your creature! I know! Next you'll be asking me to come and watch your creature! Well, I can't! You know that! So stop asking!'

'I only want to be friends –'

'Oh, go buy a burger!'

'But –'

'Bye!'

19

'You're two tokens short of a toaster!'

'Sob!'

'Stop crying, Dillon.'

'Sob!'

'Oh, get out!'

20

Dillon sat on the doorstep still going –

'Sob!'

And heard –

Chomp!

Splash!

Gurgle!

'Eeeee!'

Who wants to see Hooligan's creature anyway? I don't! Who cares if it goes chomp? I don't! Who cares if it makes Hooligan go 'Eeeee!'? I don't! I don't care about anything –

'Don't cry,' said the Hooligan, tapping Dillon's shoulder.

'Ooooo – you made me jump! And if you've come over here to say anything nasty, then you can just go straight back home –'

'I haven't come to say anything nasty. I've come to give you yet another present.' The Hooligan handed him a small bottle of bright-pink liquid. 'It's my shampoo,' she said. Then, noticing Dillon's confused look, continued, 'Well, you *did* say you liked the smell. And your hair *is* a bit of a mess. All tangled with daydreams, I shouldn't wonder. So I thought . . . well, the shampoo might do some untangling.'

'You're always giving me presents. Why?'

'Well . . . to be honest, I'm finding it hard to enjoy my

creature, knowing you're sad. I know it sounds wishy-washy! But I can't help it!'

And with that, the Hooligan dashed back into her house.

21

That night Dillon lay in bed and waited for his grandpa to fall asleep.

On his bedside cabinet was the silver watering-can.

And the bag of earth.

And the bottle of shampoo.

'Zzzzz!'

At last! thought Dillon.

He grabbed the shampoo and dashed to the bathroom.

22

I feel stupid doing this! thought Dillon, sticking his head under the tap. What can possibly happen just by washing my hair in a different shampoo? Well, that's my hair wet. Where's the bottle?

Here it is!

Unscrew the lid!

Pour shampoo on my head!

Rub it in!

It smells very strong. Much stronger than when it made Grandpa's nose hairs itch yesterday. But, then again, now it's on my head, not across the street.

Difficult to describe the smell.

Like all the best things from far-away places mixed together.

Aha! Some soap's in my eyes! Ooooo!

Best rinse them with water . . .

That's better.

Oh, look! The bathroom's full of bubbles. Like being in a washing-machine.

Now . . . rinse my hair.

That's it!

Hair all clean and free of tangles.

But . . . that's all!

Nothing else is happening!

Oh, well . . . back to bed.

23

As Dillon lay in bed the smell of the shampoo hovered round him.

He felt very peaceful and calm.

And, that night, he dreamed . . .

24

I'm in a desert! Nothing but sand everywhere. And the sun's very hot! Hotter than I've ever felt it. Like being in an oven.

Phew! I'm sweating! It's trickling down my face. And my back.

I'm so thirsty.

But there's nothing to drink! Just sand and sand and –

Wait! What's that? Something on the sand up ahead. It's the size of a billiard ball and –

It's a tangerine!

Perfect! I can drink its juice.

Mmm . . . delicious. That's quenched my thirst. I only hope it doesn't put hairs on my nose.

Ahhh! The sun is really burning my skin. Now I know what it feels like to be a slice of bread in a toaster.

I wish I had something to soothe the burning –

Wait! What's that?

A bottle of something in the sand up ahead. It looks like a milk bottle –

That's because it is! Milk! Perfect! I can soothe my skin with it.

Mmm . . . that feels better. I only hope it doesn't put warts on my chin.

Ooooo! The sun's setting now! Getting colder by the second.

Look! Now it's night! I'm freezing.

I wish I had something to keep me warm –

Wait! What's this?

A blanket! Perfect! I'll wrap it round me.

Mmm . . . I'm as snug as a bug in a rug. I only hope it doesn't wrinkle me from tip to toe –

Wait! What's that?

Something in the sand –

It's a flower!

A large white bloom with multicoloured specks.

It's so beautiful!

Let's pick the –

25

'– Flower!' said Dillon, waking.

It was morning now and sunlight streamed through the window.

The clock on the bedside cabinet told Dillon that he had overslept by almost two hours.

I've never done that before! he thought with surprise.

And then he saw something even more surprising.

Something that made him gasp out loud.

Because in his hand was the flower.

26

It can't be! thought Dillon. How can I dream a flower, then still have it when I'm awake? It's just not possible –

'DILLON – TISHOO!'

Dillon stared at the flower.

Then at the silver watering-can.

Then the bag of earth.

'DILLON – TISHOO!'

And suddenly he knew what to do.

27

'Where have you been, Dillon? I've been calling and calling! My sore throat is red raw now! And my sneezing has given me a headache. And my shivering's rattled the dentures from my head – What are you doing?'

'Pouring this bag of earth on to your bed, Grandpa.'

'Why?'

'I'm not sure yet.'

'Wh-what are you doing now?'

'Planting this flower in the earth, Grandpa.'

'Why?'

'I'm not sure yet.'

'Wh-wh-what are you doing now?'

'Watering the flower with this silver watering-can.'

'Why?'

'I'm not sure yet.'

'B-b-but look at the state of my bed, Dillon. It's earthy and wet with a flower sticking out of it! Not even a monkey would be this stupid! Even a lettuce leaf would have more sense. You must be more tokens short of a toaster than I ever realized –'

'SHUT UP, GRANDPA!' Dillon suddenly yelled. 'YOU'RE A SELFISH OLD MAN WHO HAS NO REASON TO BE BEDRIDDEN AT ALL!'

And that's when it happened!

28

The flower on the bed sprouted another flower.

Then another flower.

Then another.

Another!

'Wh-what's happening, Dillon?'

'Something remarkable.'

Now stalks and leaves were sprouting.

And on every stalk were more flowers.

And those flowers sprouted more stalks.

And those stalks more flowers.

And more.

More!

Their scent filled the room.

'DILLON!'

And that's when the stalks lifted the bed into the air . . .

29

'Ahhhhh!' cried Grandpa, falling out of the bed.

He landed with a thump on the floor.

The floor that was now covered with –

Yellow flowers!

Blue flowers!

Pink flowers!

And now the flowers were spilling out of the room.

Going into the hallway.

Up walls!

Down stairs!

Across ceilings!

Filling the house!

'Scary!' gasped Grandpa. Then sniffed a nearby bloom. 'And beautiful!'

30

When the flowers had filled the house they stopped growing.

Grandpa got to his feet and looked round.

Slowly, he stepped out into the hall.

'Orchids,' Grandpa said, his eyes full of wonder. 'That's what the flowers are called. I used to grow them when I was a gardener. Years ago. Before you were born! Oh . . . look at them!' His voice was softer and gentler than Dillon had ever heard it. 'They need so much looking after. You have to tend to their every whim day and night.' He grinned very wide. 'What fun!'

'Can I go out and play with Hooligan now, Grandpa?' asked Dillon.

'Of course, Dillon,' replied Grandpa, kissing the top of his grandson's head. 'And I'm sorry if I've been a grumpy old so-and-so for most of your life. Things will change from now on. I promise you!' Another kiss. 'You go and enjoy yourself, while I tend my favourite flowers in all the world!'

31

Knock! Knock!

The Hooligan opened the door. 'You're just in time,' she said to Dillon, holding a hamburger in the air. 'Feeding time!'

She led him to her room.

A large fish-tank was in the corner.

In the tank was a multicoloured fish with sharp teeth.

'What is it?' asked Dillon.

'A piranha,' she told him. 'Watch!'

The Hooligan dropped the hamburger into the water.

The piranha darted at the raw meat.

Sharp teeth flashed.

Bubbles erupted!

Chomp!

Gurgle!

Slurp!

'Eeeee!' went the Hooligan, holding Dillon's hand.

'Eeeee!' went Dillon, holding the Hooligan's hand.

Cover illustration by Mark Longworth. Inside illustrations by Steve Lee

Neil Arksey

from MacB

'Oi, Goldilocks!'

Shanice. Banksie watched his sister approach, flanked by two girlfriends.

'That was *us* your stupid friend nearly hit with a can.'

Dark-eyed Nina shook her raven curls. Cropped tomboy, Eve, chewed gum.

'It just missed Nina's head.'

Mac was smirking.

'Your friend is a *turnip.*'

'Total.' Banksie tapped his skull. 'He can't help it.'

'You might at least teach the idiot some manners,' said Shanice, 'if you're going to hang around with him.' She glowered at Mac. 'Too cool to say sorry, I suppose?'

Mac shrugged.

Shanice shook her head and turned to her brother. 'So, sampled anything exciting?'

'The rifle range . . .'

'Intrepid!' Shanice laughed. 'Is that *it*?'

Banksie felt himself blush. 'Yeah, so far – apart from toffee apples and hot dogs.'

'The rifle range!' Shanice turned to her girlfriends. 'What is it about boys and guns? Adventurous, or what!'

Eve and Nina shook their heads.

'The Big Wheel.' Shanice pointed. 'The Wall of

Death, the Skydiver – haven't you been on *any* rides?'

Mac snorted. 'Kids' stuff.'

'Oh really, danger-boy?' Shanice turned. 'Too tame for you? Not up to the thrills of blindly kicking cans in the dark?'

Mac shrugged.

'He's so tough!' purred Nina.

Eve growled. 'I bet he had *mustard* on his hot-dog!'

'Are you kidding?' Shanice made wide eyes. 'This guy has chilli on his breakfast!'

The girls laughed.

Stifling a grin, Banksie glanced at his mate. Shanice and her friends could rip the best to shreds. If only Mac would keep his mouth shut.

'Put it this way –' Mac jabbed the air with his finger – 'nothing at this fair could scare me.'

Shanice glanced at her girlfriends. 'Is that a fact?'

Mac puffed out his chest. 'Uh-huh.'

Shanice studied him. 'Ever been to a fortune teller?'

Mac snorted. 'You're joking, aren't you? Gypsy Rosa Lee?'

'No, actually,' said Shanice, 'I'm not joking. And no, it isn't Gypsy Rosa *anything*.' Her eyes pierced. 'Oh, but fortune telling's kids' stuff too, I suppose?' She aimed an imaginary gun at Mac's chest. 'Mr Reckless Cool . . . ' Slowly, she tightened her finger on the invisible trigger. 'Mr Sharp Shooter . . .'

PooOOSssssh!

'He flinched!' shrieked Nina.

'It was a *twitch*,' snapped Mac.

'You practically *jumped*.' Shanice laughed, pointing. 'At

some hydraulic, hissing thing on that ride!'

The girls' shrill laughter rose above the noise of the fair.

Mac folded his arms across his chest.

Shanice walked over. 'What are you afraid of, danger-boy?' She spoke quietly, just inches from his face.

'Nothing.'

They stared.

'Really!' Shanice shook her head, smiled and leant closer. 'Then go visit the fortune teller. Go on, if you're so fearless. I *dare* you. Here –' she placed a five-pound note on his folded arms – 'you and my brother. My treat!'

Mac screwed up the note and flung it back.

Letters painted large on the side of the caravan spelt: DESTINY.

At the top of the steps, Mac paused and peered inside. 'This is *your* doing.'

Banksie shook his head. 'Dug your own grave, mate.'

'You agreed with your sister!'

'It was hard not to, the way you were carrying on. Anyway she owed me a fiver.'

Mac scowled and stepped inside.

Banksie followed. The room was small. There were chairs, the lighting was dim.

Mac sniffed. '*Ugh!*' He pulled a face.

'Incense,' explained Banksie. He recognized the smell from his sister's bedroom.

'I was expecting you . . .'

Both boys jumped. The voice, a woman's, came from behind a bead curtain.

'Please . . . come through, boys.'

Banksie returned Mac's stare. Pulling aside the beaded strands, he bowed to his friend. 'After you.'

They entered.

The small, dark room was strangely, eerily hushed, as if the fairground noises had been somehow absorbed by the gloom.

'Soundproofing.' A candle flickered. The owner of the warm, husky voice stepped out from behind a partition. The candle moved with her, lighting her face – strong cheekbones, full lips, glistening braids. She smiled, lowering the candle in a gesture towards the table. 'Please – come and sit. Make yourselves at home.'

'How did you . . .?' Mac sounded edgy.

The woman laughed, gently. 'Read your mind?'

Mac nodded.

'It was an easy guess. The fairground's noisy – silence is the first thing strangers notice when they enter. I need peace for my work.' Reaching up, she adjusted the light above the table. It hissed; its soft greenish glow grew brighter, pushing back the shadows. 'Gas*sss*light . . .' The hiss of her voice mingled with the hiss of the gas. 'Limelight – so much prettier and friendlier than electric, don't you think? Please – sit.'

Banksie gave his friend a nudge. He pulled back a chair. 'You knew we were coming,' he said.

The woman's smile broadened, showing large white teeth. 'Let's say, I had an inkling.'

The teeth were like tombstones. Banksie stared – the woman's widening eyes began to *glow* a strange green colour. He gulped.

'Don't be alarmed,' the woman chuckled, 'my contact

lenses catch the light.'

Banksie felt his stomach tighten.

Mac shifted in his seat. 'So –' he cleared his throat – 'no crystal ball?'

The woman shook her head. 'I've never shown much affinity.' She cupped an imaginary ball with her hands. 'Basic ball skills can be picked up so easily, don't you think? But real talent's a different matter – either you've got it, or you haven't.'

Banksie felt the eyes flicker – from Mac to him, and back again. An eyebrow arched.

'Wouldn't you agree?'

Mac opened his mouth, but there was no sound. He nodded.

She chuckled softly. 'Oh, I have *talent*, but not the sort that works through crystal. Eyes and hands are my tools.' She rubbed her palms together in a slow, circular action, smooth and rhythmical. 'Magic is all around us, it suffuses the globe. I've borrowed here and there, from everywhere: Voodoo, Obeah, African, Romany, Druid. I stick to the bedrock stuff: dice, runes, tarot, lifelines.'

The movement of the woman's hands was hypnotic. She turned her palms upwards and spread her forearms on the table. Her skin glowed warm mahogany against the darker wood.

'A seer must be versatile. She needs to be fluid. She's a medium. Spirits speak *through* her and *to* her.' The fingers beckoned. 'Give your hands to Hecate.'

Mac frowned.

'My spirit name,' said the woman, stretching her hands closer. 'Come.'

Banksie and Mac each took hold of a hand.

'Each other's too,' she said. 'Now – of what do you wish to learn: past, present or future?'

Mac and Banksie glanced at one another.

'All three?' said Banksie.

'You may choose only one.'

'Then it's got to be the future,' said Mac. 'We know about the past and the present.'

The woman nodded. Slowly, she bowed her head. 'If, whilst I'm talking, I describe anything either of you recognize as having relevance, squeeze my hand to let me know.'

Banksie felt a faint tingling sensation where her palm touched his. A moment later . . . the same feeling only fainter in his other palm. Mac was staring wide-eyed – he had felt it too.

'I sense . . .' said the woman, '. . . I sense a tight-knit group of boys . . . they're wearing uniforms . . . no, rather they are uniformly dressed . . . a gang . . . or perhaps more organized than that – a *team*? Yes, some kind of team.'

Banksie squeezed.

'Aah!' The woman raised her head and gave a low chuckle. 'Both of you recognize this image. That's good. I'm on the right track.' She inclined her head once more. 'I'll try to go deeper. Please shut your eyes. Focus your mind. Let us see what we can find.'

As Banksie closed his eyes, the gas lamp's hiss seemed to grow louder. He fought the urge to fidget. His arms felt heavy, he wanted to stretch and flex them. The woman's hand felt hot; Mac's felt like ice. Taking a long slow breath, he tried to obey the request to 'focus'. The school team – was Mac concentrating on it too? He had to be. Getting in that team meant *everything.*

'The team,' said the woman, 'is a football team.'

Banksie squeezed her hand again.

'There are lots of boys . . . all eager to join, it's very important to them. It's very important to you. Competition is fierce.'

'Do we get in?' blurted Mac.

'I see you playing . . .' said the woman.

'We play all the time,' said Banksie. 'What are we wearing?'

'What colour shirts?' said Mac.

'Let me see . . .' said the woman. 'How strange . . . the shirts don't seem to have colour.'

'No colour?' said Banksie. 'But we *are* wearing shirts? Could it be they're white?'

The woman made a tutting noise. 'Of course! How foolish of me! That's why – the sun is shining and the shirts you're both wearing are dazzling white.'

'St Dunstan's!' said Mac.

Banksie felt Mac pinch his hand. He sneaked a glance. Mac winked then shut his eyes again.

'The team's captain,' muttered the woman, 'has to be replaced.'

'Replaced . . .' echoed Mac, '. . . who by?' He leant forward, barely able to contain his excitement. 'Who comes after him? Can you see? Is it one of *us*?'

The woman frowned. 'Both of you.'

'Both?'

'Going deeper now . . .' said the woman, 'further into

your future, deeper into your destiny . . .' Her frown sharpened; darkened.

Banksie closed his eyes.

'The field won't always be so sunny . . .' A graver tone had crept into her voice. 'I see shadows lurking. I see storm clouds gathering. There is mud now . . . and *blood* on those pure-white shirts.'

Banksie felt himself tense.

'*Blood* . . .' The woman groaned. '. . . *and mud. Mud and blood!*' Her voice had become a low, rumbling rasp. '*Beneath this table*,' she muttered, '*below our feet, lies a point where two paths meet.*' The rhythm of her words grew stronger, like a chant. '*Where ley lines cross, they double force. Now let this power reveal your course.*'

The gas lamp's background hiss seemed to swell. Banksie's heart was racing. He glanced at Mac. Wasn't there a new sound, a whisper in that hiss? Mac's eyes were open again too, he was listening for something.

'*Mud and blood . . . blood and mud!*'

Banksie peered. Was that the woman's voice? Her lips weren't moving.

'*Against all odds, two friends hold sway*
Giants on the field till the darkest day.
One captains first, the other thereafter
One burns fiercest, the other – brighter.'

A sharp gust of wind buffeted the caravan. The gas lamp extinguished with a pop.

'*Blood and mud* . . .' gasped the voice in the darkness, '. . . *mud and blood!*'

Gillian Cross

from The Demon Headmaster

It was a big playground, full of groups of strange children. No one so much as glanced at Dinah and she felt very awkward. But she was not a person who showed her feelings. Her pinched mouth did not relax for a moment. She looked round, wondering if there were any games she could join in. She thought there would be football, skipping and He. And lots of people shouting and telling the latest crazy jokes from Friday night's Eddy Hair Show.

But it was not like that at all. All the children were standing in small neat circles in different parts of the playground, muttering. Carefully Dinah sidled up to the first circle, trying to catch what the voices were saying. When she heard, she could hardly believe it.

'Nine twenty-ones are a hundred and eighty-nine,

Ten twenty-ones are two hundred and ten,

Eleven twenty-ones are two hundred and thirty-one . . .'

Extraordinary! She left them to it and moved across to another group, wondering if they were doing something more interesting. But they seemed to be reciting too. Only what they were saying was different.

'William the First 1066 to 1087,
William the Second 1087 to 1100,
Henry the First 1100 to 1135 . . .'

She stood beside them for some time, but they did not waver or look round at her. They just went on chanting, their faces earnest. Behind her she could hear a third group. There, the children were muttering the names of the capitals of different countries.

'The capital of France is Paris,
The capital of Spain is Madrid,
The capital of the United States is –'

'New York,' said a little girl's voice.

'Lucy!' A bigger girl took her by the shoulder and shook her. 'You know that's not right. Come on, quickly. What is it?'

'I can't – I can't remember,' Lucy said in a scared voice. 'You know I've been away. Tell me. Please, Julie.'

'You know we're not supposed to tell you if you haven't learnt it,' Julie said crossly. 'Now come on. The capital of the United States is –'

Miserably, Lucy chewed at her bottom lip and shook her head from side to side. 'I can't remember.'

The whole circle of children was looking accusingly at her and Dinah was suddenly annoyed with them for being so smug. Stepping forwards, she whispered in Lucy's ear, 'It's Washington DC.'

'The capital of the United States is Washington DC,' Lucy gabbled, with a quick, grateful smile.

From the rest of the circle, cold, disapproving eyes glared at Dinah. *Never be too clever,* she thought. *I should've known that.* Her face pinched up tight again as she stepped back and heard them start up once more. 'The capital of Russia is Moscow. The capital of Brazil is-'

Woodenly, Dinah walked on round the playground, waiting for the bell to ring or the whistle to go.

But there was no bell. No whistle. Nothing. Instead, quite abruptly, all sounds in the playground stopped and the children turned round to stare at the school.

There on the steps stood a row of six children, three boys and three girls. They were all tall and heavily built and they were marked out from the others by a large white P sewn on to their blazer pockets. Without smiling, the tallest girl took a pace forwards.

'Form – rows!' she yelled into the silence.

'Yes, Rose,' all the children said, in perfect unison. As quietly and steadily as marching soldiers, they walked together, forming neat straight lines which ran the length of the playground. Each child stood exactly a foot behind the one in front. Each line was exactly three feet from the one next to it. Not quite sure what to do, Dinah stood by herself, a blotch of blue among the green.

The tallest boy on the steps walked forwards.

'Lead – in!' he bellowed.

'Yes, Jeff,' chorused the children.

Still in total silence, they began to march forward, row by row, up the steps and through the door into the school, their eyes fixed straight ahead and their feet moving in step. There was no giggling or whispering or pushing. The whole thing was utterly orderly, the only sound being the steady tramping of feet.

Dinah continued to stand still, watching, until the playground was almost clear. As the last line marched off, she tacked herself on to the end of it and walked towards the school. When she got to the top of the steps, Rose stuck out an arm, barring her way.

'Name?' she said briskly.

'Dinah Glass,' Dinah said. 'I'm new, and –'

'Just answer the questions,' Jeff interrupted her. 'What's that you're wearing?'

'It's my old school uniform. I –'

'Just answer the question,' he said again. There was no friendliness in his voice and as he spoke he looked not at Dinah but over her shoulder. 'It is not satisfactory. All pupils here shall wear correct green uniform. Kindly see to it.'

He looked so haughty and spoke so stiffly that Dinah was irritated.

'I don't know why you're being so bossy,' she said coldly. 'Anyone'd think you were one of the teachers, instead of a measly kid like anyone else.'

'All pupils shall obey the prefects,' chanted Rose, in the same stiff voice. 'The prefects are the voice of the Headmaster.'

Dinah felt puzzled, but she was determined not to show it. She thrust her chin up and looked straight at them. 'Well, I think you should take me to see the Headmaster. I've got a letter for him.'

The prefects looked doubtfully at each other. Then Jeff vanished inside the school, while the others stood barring Dinah's way. It had grown colder and the icy wind was turning her fingers blue. She lifted them to blow on them.

'Hands by your sides,' Rose rapped out instantly.

'Good deportment is the sign of an orderly mind.'

Stubbornly, Dinah went on blowing. At once, Rose said, 'Sarah! Simon!'

Dinah's hands were instantly seized by two of the other prefects, who forced them down to her sides and stood holding them like that until Jeff reappeared.

'The Headmaster will see you,' he said. 'Follow me.'

Thoroughly bewildered now, Dinah walked into the school after him and along a straight corridor. At her old school, all the walls had been covered with pictures and drawings done by the pupils, but these walls were completely blank, except for a framed notice hung halfway along. Dinah swivelled her head to read it as she passed.

The man who can keep order can rule the world.

Frowning slightly, she went on following Jeff until he came to a stop in front of a door which had the single word HEADMASTER painted on it.

He knocked.

'Come in.'

Jeff pushed the door open and waved Dinah inside, pulling it shut behind her.

As she stepped through, Dinah glanced quickly round the room. It was the tidiest office she had ever seen. There were no papers, no files, no pictures on the walls. Just a large, empty-topped desk, a filing cabinet and a bookcase with a neat row of books.

She took it all in in one second and then forgot it as her eyes fell on the man standing by the window. He was tall and thin, dressed in an immaculate black suit. From his shoulders, a long, black teacher's gown hung in heavy folds, like wings, giving him the appearance of a huge crow. Only his head was startlingly white. Fair hair, almost as colourless as snow, lay round a face with paper-white skin and pallid lips. His eyes were hidden behind dark glasses. like two black holes in the middle of all the whiteness.

She cleared her throat. 'Hallo. I'm Dinah Glass and I –'

He raised a long, ivory-coloured hand. 'Please do not speak until you are asked. Idle chatter is an inefficient waste of energy.'

Unnervingly, he went on staring at her for a moment or two without saying anything else. Dinah wished she could see the eyes behind the dark lenses. With his eyes hidden, his expression was unreadable.

Finally, he waved a hand towards an upright chair, pulled round to face the desk. 'Sit down.' He sat down himself, facing her, and pulled a sheet of paper out of a drawer.

'Dinah Glass,' he said crisply, writing it down in neat, precise script. 'You are being fostered by Mrs Hunter?'

Dinah nodded.

'Answer properly, please.'

'Yes, sir.'

'And why is she not here, to introduce you?'

'She couldn't come, but she's sent you a letter.'

Reaching across the desk, the Headmaster twitched it out of her hand and slit the envelope with a small steel paper knife. As he read the letter, Dinah settled herself more comfortably, expecting to be asked a string of questions.

But there were no questions. Instead, he pushed a sheet of paper across the desk towards her. 'This is a test,' he said. 'It is given to all new pupils.'

'Haven't you got a report on me?' Dinah said. 'From my other school?'

'No one else's reports are of any use to me,' said the Headmaster. 'Please be quiet and do the test.'

His voice was low, but somehow rather frightening. Dinah took a pen out of her pocket and looked down at the paper.

The questions were fairly hard. Mostly sums, with a bit of English thrown in and one or two brain-teasers. She knew that most children would have found them difficult to answer and she paused for a moment, working out where she was going to make her deliberate mistakes. Not too many. Just enough to avoid trouble.

Then she picked up the pen and began to write. As she scribbled, she could feel him watching her and every time she glanced up he was the same. Pale and motionless, with two black circles where his eyes should have been. She was so nervous that she stumbled once or twice, getting some of the answers right where she had meant to make mistakes. To keep the balance, she had to botch up all the last three questions. Not very good. It did not look as convincing as it should have done. Her hand trembled slightly as she passed the paper back across the table.

The Headmaster scanned it carefully for a moment, then looked up at her.

'You are an intelligent girl.'

Dinah's heart sank, but, with an effort, she kept her

face calm, meeting the Headmaster's gaze steadily. At last, he said, 'But you make too many mistakes. I wonder –' He chewed for a moment on his bottom lip. Then he shrugged. 'It doesn't matter. I dare say we shall find out all about you in due course.'

She looked down to the floor, trying not to seem too relieved, and waiting to be told which class she should go to. But the Headmaster did not seem in any hurry to get rid of her. He crumpled the test paper in his hand and dropped it into the rubbish bin. Then, slowly, he reached up a hand to take off his glasses.

Dinah found herself shivering. Ridiculously, she expected him to have pink eyes, because the rest of his face was so colourless. Or perhaps no eyes at all . . .

But his eyes were not pink. They were large and luminous, and a peculiar sea-green colour. She had never seen eyes like them before, and she found herself staring into them. Staring and staring.

'Funny you should be so tired,' he said, softly. 'So early in the morning.'

She opened her mouth to say that she was not tired, but, to her surprise, she yawned instead.

'*So* tired,' crooned the Headmaster, his huge, extraordinary eyes fixed on her face. 'You can hardly move your arms and legs. You are so tired, so tired. You feel your head begin to nod and slowly, slowly your eyes are starting to close. *So* tired and sleepy.'

He's mad, Dinah thought muzzily. *The whole school's raving mad.* But she felt her eyes start to close, in spite of all she could do. She was drifting, drifting . . . All she could see was two pools, deep green like the sea, and she seemed to sink into them as she drifted off and off . . .

She opened her eyes again and gave a nervous laugh. 'I'm sorry. What did you say?'

'You fell asleep,' the Headmaster said coldly. 'You have been asleep for a long time.' He put his glasses on again.

'Asleep?' Dinah stared.

'For the whole morning.'

She looked at him in bewilderment and then glanced round at the clock on the wall. To her amazement, the hands pointed to twelve o'clock. 'But I don't understand.'

'Perhaps you should go to bed earlier,' he said, with a strange smile. 'Now go and have some dinner. The dining hall is at the end of this corridor. After dinner, you will go into the Hall with Class One.'

Still puzzled, Dinah nodded.

The Headmaster looked disagreeably at her. 'Your uniform,' he said, 'is not what I require.'

'It's what I had for my other school. When I was at the Children's Home.'

His lips narrowed. 'I dislike argument. It serves no useful purpose. You will appear in the correct school uniform by next Monday. I am sending a list to Mrs Hunter to ensure that she buys the proper items. I like to see all my pupils dressed in an orderly manner.' His voice rose a tone. 'I will not *endure* disorder. It is inefficient. Now go and have some dinner.'

Shakily, Dinah stood up and made for the door. As she reached out her hand for the handle, the Headmaster spoke again.

'I have put you in the same class as Lloyd Hunter, but

I wish you to have as little as possible to do with Lloyd and Harvey. They are not a good example. They do not fit in at this school.'

'That –' Dinah had been going to say that it would be difficult. But just in time she remembered that he did not like argument. Better to be quiet and obey. Until she had had time to think everything over, to try and work out why the school was so strange. 'Yes, sir,' she murmured.

As she went out and shut the door, her head was humming with thoughts. Asleep? All the morning? It did not make sense. And had the Headmaster simply sat and stared at her all that time, without trying to wake her up? She shuddered and put a finger into her mouth to suck it thoughtfully.

Something made her take the finger out again and look at it. It was sore. There was a small red patch at one end, as if a pin had been driven into it. But she did not remember having pricked her finger. Frowning, she walked along the corridor towards the dining hall.

Anne Fine

Fight the Good Fight

Both my daughters hate *the smell of cigarette smoke. (Like my heroine's granny, I've a soft spot for it myself.) I was used to hearing them grumble about it each time they came home from school on the city bus, and wrote this story to show that I was really on their side.*

Authors often write to try to alter something in society. So we can have mixed feelings when things change, in case our work looks a little out of date. But the best *part of us wants to cheer that the world can change so much so quickly. So enjoy a little bit of history!*

'I've heard of fighting the good fight,' the bus driver says to me almost every morning when I get off, 'but you are really weird.' He shakes his head. 'Really weird.'

He's quite wrong. I'm perfectly *normal.* There's nothing *wrong* with me. I'm probably about the same age as you. I'm probably about as clever, and I can take a joke, just like you. The only thing different about me is that I hate cigarette smoke. I just can't stand it. I think it stinks.

It's only the smell of it I hate. I quite like the way it looks. I used to love sitting on my mum's knee, watching the wispy streams of fine blue smoke float up from her fag ends (before I frightened her into giving up with all my talk of 'coughin' nails'). I liked the way that, when she moved, or laughed, or waved her hand as she was talking, the smoke would twist and wind on its way up to the ceiling, and you could blow on it gently, till it drifted into great billowing circles.

And I liked watching my dad smoke his pipe, too (before he threw it in the rubbish after I saw a smoker's lungs on telly, all brown and kippery, and burst into tears). I liked the way he puffed out huge silvery-blue clouds, and smacked his lips, making little putt-put-putt noises, whenever he thought it might be going out. He was an ace pipe-smoker, my dad – a real professional. He once kept it going all the way home from my granny's in a rainstorm.

Granny's the only one of my relations who smokes now (when she can stop coughing long enough to take a good puff). But since I only see her every other Saturday, I don't really mind.

What I mind is the bus.

My bus, the number 14, runs from one end of the city to the other. It's only a single decker, so in the mornings it gets terribly crowded, partly with people like me going to school, and partly with adults on their way to work. By the time the bus reaches my stop, Railton Dyke End, at ten past eight, there's hardly ever any seats left. I usually have to stand for fifteen minutes, till I get off at the end of Great Barr Street. And the bus is sometimes so crowded I get pushed further and further down the gangway.

And that's the problem. That's why the bus driver thinks I'm so weird. I can't stand moving further down the gangway. The front half of the bus is fine by me. It's all non-smoking, with little red stickers saying so on the windows, and nothing but clean bright-green peppermint wrappers stuffed in the ashtrays, and even a sign on the glass pane behind the driver's back that says *Have a heart – Stop smoking now.* But the back of the bus is disgusting. It's all grey-faced men and women wheezing and coughing and spluttering out clouds of their filthy-smelling grey smoke, and flicking their dirty ash flakes on one another's clothing, and leaving their fag ends smouldering in the overflowing ashtrays, and trampling their nasty little soggy yellow stubs on the floor in their hurry to get off the bus at the right stop, and light up another.

It's horrible. I hate it. I wouldn't mind so much if the smell stayed down their end with them, and you could turn your back on the whole revolting spectacle and just pretend it wasn't there. But not only does stale smoke drift up to our end, but sometimes when the bus gets really crowded, the driver even tries to force you to move further along and stand at the filthy end, stop after stop, while the vile smell seeps into your clothes and your hair, and even your skin.

'Move along inside. Move down the bus, *please.* You, too.' (He means me.)

'Did you hear what the driver said, little girl? Make room. Move along a bit.'

I cling desperately to the rail of the last pair of non-smoking seats.

'Sorry, I can't move down any further. That's the smoking end, and I don't smoke.'

Sometimes people glare. Sometimes they mutter. But, mostly, they just stare at me as if I were bonkers.

And I'm not. As I said at the start, I am a perfectly normal person. There's nothing weird about preferring halfway reasonable air to standing over some stranger's personal miniature chemical refinery, breathing in the waste fumes. I don't see why I should be forced to move down the bus.

'You clog up my gangway every morning,' the bus driver complains when I force my way up to the very front, to get off. 'You ought to be more co-operative.'

I don't see why. I wouldn't co-operate with putting my head in a noose. I wouldn't co-operate with throwing myself out of a helicopter without a parachute. I don't see why I should co-operate with getting my lungs black.

But when I tell him so as he slows down at the corner of the street that leads to my school, he gets all snappy with me.

'You should go through the proper channels,' he tells me. 'You should stop making trouble on my bus.'

But I'd tried proper channels. Proper channels were perfectly useless, I can tell you. I got my mother to write a letter to the bus company, and all she got back was some very polite rubbish about 'fully appreciating her point of view', but 'having to consider the feelings of the other passengers'.

Well, what about my feelings? Don't they count? I catch the bus every single morning we have school. I have for years. That's over two hundred times a year. That's over a thousand bus rides *already*. I'd have to be a real drip not to fight back. So, over the years, I have developed my own private methods of making people stub their cigarettes out on the bus. (That's what the driver means by 'making trouble'.)

My first method is the best. It works the quickest, especially on motherly women with lots of shopping bags who are having their first quiet fag of the morning. Just as my victim lights up and leans back, sighing with pleasure, I lean towards her and, tugging a grubby old paper tissue out of my pocket, I start to snivel. If my victim doesn't notice, I sob a bit, quietly, and start my shoulders heaving up and down. I try to get real tears rolling down my cheeks, but that only tends to work if I get in the cigarette's slipstream.

After less than a minute the victim always asks kindly: 'Are you crying, little girl? What's the matter?'

'Nothing.'

I wipe my nose on the back of my hand, but sweetly, like a small child in a family film, not disgustingly, like Gareth Chatterton in primary four.

The victim leans forward and whispers: 'Come on, dear. You can tell me. Are you hurt?' I shake my head.

'In trouble?'

'No-oo.'

'Is anyone at school picking on you?'

'No,' I say. 'It's not that. It's –' I make my voice tremble. And then I hesitate, so she has to ask again.

'What is it, dear?'

Then I look her straight in the eye.

'It's my aunty,' I say. 'She used to smoke, too. The same brand as you. But now she's got –' I pause, and watch the cigarette as it burns away between her fingers. Then, while the little word I'm *not* saying rings an alarm bell in my victim's brain, I finish up delicately: 'Well, she's very ill. She can hardly breathe now.'

At this point the victim always stubs out her fag, and looks thoughtfully at the little cardboard packet in her hand. I don't feel guilty. Why should I? Better she's my victim than the cigarette's, after all. And when it comes to getting a bit of fresh air on our bus, every quick stub-out helps.

I used this method a lot in the beginning. It worked a treat. The only problem was that the bus tends to carry the same passengers, day after day, so after a week or two only new passengers bothered to ask me why I was so unhappy.

So I moved on to method number two.

'I can smell fire!'

'Fire?'

'Fire!'

Everyone holds their fags up a little bit higher, and inspects them carefully. Then they inspect the folds in their clothing, and peer down between the bags and briefcases on the floor, to see if a burning cigarette has set something smouldering.

'Really. I can smell something burning. Can't you smell it? It's very strong.'

'It's just the cigarette smoke, dear.'

'Oh, no,' I argue. 'It couldn't just be cigarette smoke. It smells *disgusting*, and it's getting *worse*.'

One by one, people at the back are getting nervous and stubbing out their cigarettes just that little bit early.

'I can still smell it. I'm sure everyone can. There is a definite smell of burning. It's terribly strong, and very nasty.'

Sometimes I can get every single passenger at the back of the bus neatly stubbed out before we even reach the Safeway at the bottom of Dean Bank.

Then there's method number three. That's when I double over in a coughing fit, and make my face go pink, then red, then blue if it isn't Monday and I feel up to it. I cough and cough. I make a simply appalling noise. You'd think it was my lungs getting destroyed, not theirs. It sobers them up pretty quickly, I can tell you. Whole bus loads can't stub out fast enough when I get going.

Method number four is a variation on number three. It's just a combination of coughing and glaring. I use it when there's only one smoker left who's pretending my coughing fit is nothing to do with their smoking.

Method number five only works with women. I brush imaginary ash off my clothes. I brush and brush away, eyeing the cigarette, and soon the woman tries holding her fag in a different position. But I just keep on brushing. And in the end she begins to think that, wherever she holds it, her ash is going to float on to my clothing. Defeated, she stubs it out.

Now and then, miraculously, there's a free seat. If it's up the front, I take it. If it's at the back, I ignore it. I'd rather stand. But if it's in the last row between the smokers and the non-smokers, I take it and turn round to start conversations.

'Is that the brand with the coupons that get you the free iron lung?'

'Have you smoked for long?' (That always depresses them. They always have.)

If I've got a snack for my break-time, I start to unwrap it. Then I turn round and say: 'I hope my eating my granola bar isn't going to spoil your cigarette.'

Or I might kneel on the seat, lean over, and chat away merrily.

'We're doing a project on smoking at school. Did you know that there are over a thousand poisons in every cigarette? Did you know that one hundred thousand people every year die earlier than they should because they smoke? Did you know that if you live in the same house as smokers, you get to smoke eighty cigarettes a year without even having one? Did you know . . .'

Everyone at the back of the bus hates me. They all complain about me when they get off.

'That child's a real pain,' they say to the driver. 'She shouldn't be allowed to travel on this bus.'

He passes their sentiments on while I'm standing by his shoulder, waiting for my stop.

'They say you're a nuisance,' he tells me.

'Me?' I say, outraged. '*I'm* the nuisance? I like that!'

'There's not much to choose between you.'

'There most certainly is,' I argue. 'I'll tell you what there is to choose between us. If *they* stopped, *I'd* stop, straight away. If *I* stopped, they'd get *worse.* So I'd choose *me.*'

'None the less,' said the driver, 'I've had more than enough complaints. And until the company changes the rules, smokers are supposed to be welcome on this bus.' (You'll notice he didn't say they *were.* He only said they were *supposed* to be.) 'So, any more trouble from you, young lady, and I put you off at the next corner. Understand?'

Word travels faster than the number 14 bus, I can tell you. By the next morning, everyone knew that I was on probation. I only turned round once, and said quite amiably to the fellow behind me: 'Did you know smokers can get gangrene?' and the bus practically *screeched* to a halt. Before I knew what had happened I was standing on the pavement with my book bag and my gym shoes and my tennis racket and my lunch box and my English folder and my choir music and a huge bag of dress-ups for the class play.

'I did warn you,' said the driver as the automatic doors went 'phut' in my face. 'Don't try to say I didn't warn you.'

I was twenty-five minutes late. Twenty-five minutes! I tried sneaking in the back way, but it was no use because, by the time I crept up the stairs to my classroom, Mrs Phillips had taken the register and marked me absent.

'Twenty-five minutes!' she scolded. 'Absolutely disgraceful. Be late again this week, and you'll be in big trouble.'

I really tried to keep quiet on the bus the next morning. It wasn't my fault I was forced so far down the gangway that I ended up standing over some fat old fellow who could scarcely *breathe.*

He spoke to me first if you can call it speaking. It was more of a painful wheeze, really. He took his packet out of his pocket, opened it, peeped longingly at all the little killers inside, and closed it up again.

Then he glanced up and saw me watching him.

'Trying to give up,' he explained. 'Doctor's orders.'

Well, I had to say *something,* didn't I? I was only being *polite.*

'You can do it!' I encouraged him. 'You can. You can! Fight the good fight! There are eleven million ex-smokers walking around Britain with good clean lungs. You can be the eleven millionth and first!'

That's *all I said.* And it wasn't him who got all shirty. It was the others who sent word up the gangway that I should be put off the bus again – all those not under doctor's orders. Yet.

'Enjoy the walk,' said the driver, pressing the button to shut the bus doors in my face. 'Phut'.

'Bye,' I said.

It wasn't so bad that morning. I only had my book bag and my lunch box and my recorder and my project on Witchcraft and my homemade peephole camera to carry. So I was only twenty minutes late.

'I did warn you,' said Mrs Phillips. 'That's a detention. You're twenty minutes late, so I want you in tomorrow twenty minutes early. You can write me an essay.' She fished about for a title that would do nicely for a punishment: 'I know. *A Business Letter.* And I want it properly set out and neatly written, with perfect spelling.'

I know when I'm beaten. I didn't argue. I just got up twenty minutes earlier the next morning, and caught the bus that comes twenty minutes earlier, and reached school twenty minutes earlier, and sat down to write.

Room 14
Stocklands School
Great Barr Street

21 April

Dear Sir or Madam
I'm writing to tell you how bothered I am that some of the pupils in my class are forced to travel each morning on buses that are so thick with cigarette smoke that they arrive coughing, and with pink eyes. I have the number 14 bus particularly in mind.

In my view smoking is for kippers, and children should be smokeless zones.

Please ban smoking on single decker buses as soon as possible, particularly the number 14.

Yours faithfully

I left the space at the bottom blank. I didn't sign Mrs Phillips's name in case she thought I was being cheeky.

How was I to know she'd sweep in and scoop it up, read it through, then sign her name with a flourish in the gap I'd left? How was I to know she'd root through the clutter in her desk to find an envelope, and send me off to the office to look up the bus company's address in the telephone directory? How was I to know she'd even dig in her own purse and give me a stamp?

She saw me looking at her.

'Fight the good fight,' she said.

The reply came a week later. I was surprised to see it was a bit different from the one my mother got back from them last year. There was a lot less of the 'considering the feelings of other passengers' stuff, and a lot more about 'coming to realize the hazards of passive smoking', and 'frequent discussions on the possibility of changing bus company policy in this respect'.

'There you go,' said Mrs Phillips. 'They're half-way to cracking already. Just keep on at 'em.'

And so I do. I'm no trouble at all on the bus now I've taken to getting up five minutes earlier so I can walk two stops back and catch the bus at the Ferry Lane Factory. (A lot of people get off there, so I get a seat.) I usually sit behind the driver. I look at his *Have a heart* no smoking sign for inspiration, then I dig out one of my four letter pads, and I write my letter.

I write one letter every single morning. (Mum buys the stamps. She says it's all in a good cause.) I write for everyone I know: family, friends, shopkeepers, pen-friends, members of the gym club. Everyone signs their letter. Even Granny and the bus driver signed theirs. Granny says she wouldn't have gone to all the trouble of writing herself, being a smoker; but since I'd bothered it seemed a terrible waste not to post it. The bus driver said it's his bus and he's not allowed to smoke on it, so why should anyone else get away with it? It's not a very lofty attitude, I agree, but I didn't say anything. You see, I'm getting on a lot better with him now since I started going through the proper channels.

He still thinks I'm weird. But he helps me with my spelling if I get stuck, and he's even taken a couple of my letters home to get his wife and his sister to sign them.

And he lets me know whenever he hears rumours that all the single deckers are going non-smoking. It happens more and more often now. He thinks the change is coming. So do I. In fact, we're so sure that we've worked out which notice we're going to stick on the glass panel behind his seat on the Glorious Day. It's going to say, in big red capital letters:

WARNING
LIGHTING UP ON THIS BUS
CAN SERIOUSLY DAMAGE
YOUR HEALTH

I'll stop fighting the good fight then. But, if you see the number 14 going by, you'll still be able to recognize me. I'll be the one staring idly out of the window.

Roald Dahl

from Matilda

Matilda's brother Michael was a perfectly normal boy, but the sister, as I said, was something to make your eyes pop. By the age of *one and a half* her speech was perfect and she knew as many words as most grown-ups. The parents, instead of applauding her, called her a noisy chatterbox and told her sharply that small girls should be seen and not heard.

By the time she was *three*, Matilda had taught herself to read by studying newspapers and magazines that lay around the house. At the age of *four*, she could read fast and well and she naturally began hankering after books. The only book in the whole of this enlightened household was something called *Easy Cooking* belonging to her mother, and when she had read this from cover to cover and had learnt all the recipes by heart, she decided she wanted something more interesting.

'Daddy,' she said, 'do you think you could buy me a book?'

'A *book*?' he said. 'What d'you want a flaming book for?'

'To read, Daddy.'

'What's wrong with the telly, for heaven's sake? We've got a lovely telly with a twelve-inch screen and now you come asking for a book! You're getting spoiled, my girl!'

Nearly every weekday afternoon Matilda was left alone in the house. Her brother (five years older than her) went to school. Her father went to work and her mother went out playing bingo in a town eight miles away. Mrs Wormwood was hooked on bingo and played it five afternoons a week. On the afternoon of the day when her father had refused to buy her a book, Matilda set out all by herself to walk to the public library in the village. When she arrived, she introduced herself to the librarian, Mrs Phelps. She asked if she might sit awhile and read a book. Mrs Phelps, slightly taken aback at the arrival of such a tiny girl unacccompanied by a parent, nevertheless told her she was very welcome.

'Where are the children's books please?' Matilda asked.

'They're over there on those lower shelves,' Mrs Phelps told her. 'Would you like me to help you find a nice one with lots of pictures in it?'

'No, thank you,' Matilda said. 'I'm sure I can manage.'

From then on, every afternoon, as soon as her mother had left for bingo, Matilda would toddle down to the library. The walk took only ten minutes and this allowed her two glorious hours sitting quietly by herself in a cosy corner devouring one book after another. When she had read every single children's book in the place, she started wandering round in search of something else.

Mrs Phelps, who had been watching her with fascination for the past few weeks, now got up from her desk and went over to her. 'Can I help you, Matilda?' she asked.

'I'm wondering what to read next,' Matilda said. 'I've finished all the children's books.'

'You mean you've looked at the pictures?'

'Yes, but I've read the books as well.'

Mrs Phelps looked down at Matilda from her great height and Matilda looked right back up at her.

'I thought some were very poor,' Matilda said, 'but others were lovely. I liked *The Secret Garden* best of all. It was full of mystery. The mystery of the room behind the closed door and the mystery of the garden behind the big wall.'

Mrs Phelps was stunned. 'Exactly how old are you, Matilda?' she asked.

'Four years and three months,' Matilda said.

Mrs Phelps was more stunned than ever, but she had the sense not to show it. 'What sort of a book would you like to read next?' she asked.

Matilda said, 'I would like a really good one that grown-ups read. A famous one. I don't know any names.'

Mrs Phelps looked along the shelves, taking her time. She didn't quite know what to bring out. How, she asked herself, does one choose a famous grown-up book for a four-year-old girl? Her first thought was to pick a young teenager's romance of the kind that is written for fifteen-year-old schoolgirls, but for some reason she found herself instinctively walking past that particular shelf.

'Try this,' she said at last. 'It's very famous and very good. If it's too long for you, just let me know and I'll find something shorter and a bit easier.'

'Great Expectations,' Matilda read, 'by Charles Dickens. I'd love to try it.'

I must be mad, Mrs Phelps told herself, but to Matilda she said, 'Of course you may try it.'

Over the next few afternoons Mrs Phelps could hardly take her eyes from the small girl sitting for hour after hour in the big armchair at the far end of the room with the book on her lap. It was necessary to rest it on the lap because it was too heavy for her to hold up, which meant she had to sit leaning forward in order to read. And a strange sight it was, this tiny dark-haired person sitting there with her feet nowhere near touching the floor, totally absorbed in the wonderful adventures of Pip and old Miss Havisham and her cobwebbed house and by the spell of magic that Dickens the great story-teller had woven with his words. The only movement from the reader was the lifting of the hand every now and then to turn over a page, and Mrs Phelps always felt sad when the time came for her to cross the floor and say, 'It's ten to five, Matilda.'

During the first week of Matilda's visits Mrs Phelps had said to her, 'Does your mother walk you down here every day and then take you home?'

'My mother goes to Aylesbury every afternoon to play bingo,' Matilda had said. 'She doesn't know I come here.'

'But that's surely not right,' Mrs Phelps said. 'I think you'd better ask her.'

'I'd rather not,' Matilda said. 'She doesn't encourage reading books. Nor does my father.'

'But what do they expect you to do every afternoon in an empty house?'

'Just mooch around and watch the telly.'

'I see.'

'She doesn't really care what I do,' Matilda said a little sadly.

Mrs Phelps was concerned about the child's safety on the walk through the fairly busy village High Street and the crossing of the road, but she decided not to interfere.

Within a week, Matilda had finished *Great Expectations* which in that edition contained four hundred and eleven pages. 'I loved it,' she said to Mrs Phelps. 'Has Mr Dickens written any others?'

'A great number,' said the astounded Mrs Phelps. 'Shall I choose you another?'

Over the next six months, under Mrs Phelps's watchful and compassionate eye, Matilda read the following books:

Nicholas Nickleby by Charles Dickens
Oliver Twist by Charles Dickens
Jane Eyre by Charlotte Brontë
Pride and Prejudice by Jane Austen
Tess of the D'Urbervilles by Thomas Hardy
Gone to Earth by Mary Webb
Kim by Rudyard Kipling
The Invisible Man by H. G. Wells
The Old Man and the Sea by Ernest Hemingway
The Sound and the Fury by William Faulkner
The Grapes of Wrath by John Steinbeck
The Good Companions by J. B. Priestley
Brighton Rock by Graham Greene
Animal Farm by George Orwell

It was a formidable list and by now Mrs Phelps was filled with wonder and excitement, but it was probably a good thing that she did not allow herself to be completely carried away by it all. Almost anyone else witnessing the achievements of this small child would have been tempted to make a great fuss and shout the news all over the village and beyond, but not so Mrs Phelps. She was someone who minded her own business and had long since discovered it was seldom worth while to interfere with other people's children.

'Mr Hemingway says a lot of things I don't understand,' Matilda said to her. 'Especially about men and women. But I loved it all the same. The way he tells it I feel I am right there on the spot watching it all happen.'

'A fine writer will always make you feel that,' Mrs Phelps said. 'And don't worry about the bits you can't understand. Sit back and allow the words to wash around you, like music.'

'I will, I will.'

'Did you know', Mrs Phelps said, 'that public libraries like this allow you to borrow books and take them home?'

'I didn't know that,' Matilda said. 'Could *I* do it?'

'Of course,' Mrs Phelps said. 'When you have chosen the book you want, bring it to me so I can make a note of it and it's yours for two weeks. You can take more than one if you wish.'

From then on, Matilda would visit the library only once a week in order to take out new books and return the old ones. Her own small bedroom now became her reading-room and there she would sit and read most afternoons, often with a mug of hot chocolate beside her. She was not quite tall enough to reach things around the kitchen, but she kept a small box in the outhouse which she brought in and stood on in order to get whatever she wanted. Mostly it was hot chocolate she made, warming the milk in a saucepan on the stove before mixing it. Occasionally she made Bovril or Ovaltine. It was pleasant to take a hot drink up to her room and have it beside her as she sat in her silent room reading in the empty house in the afternoons. The books transported her into new worlds and introduced her to amazing people who lived exciting lives. She went on olden-day sailing ships with Joseph Conrad. She went to Africa with Ernest Hemingway and to India with Rudyard Kipling. She travelled all over the world while sitting in her little room in an English village.

The Amazing World of ROALD DAHL

Did you know ...?

The character of Sophie, in the story The BFG was based on his own grand-daughter Sophie Dahl.

He created the worlds of ...

and many many more in an old wooden shed in his back garden!

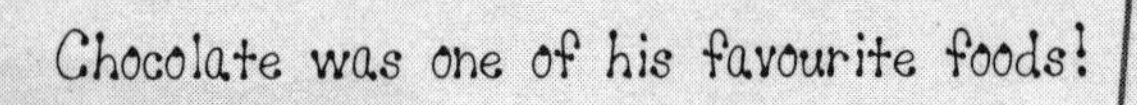

Chocolate was one of his favourite foods!

His first children's novel to be published was ...

... in 1961 (the rest is history!).

Happy Reading

Illustrations by Quentin Blake

Paul Jennings

The Spitting Rat

1

'What's a zuff?' I said to Mum.

'No such thing,' she answered. She took the letter from my hand and read it.

Dear Anthony,
I hope you like the Spitting Rat. Take it to the zough and it will bring you good luck. But whatever you doo, don't tutch it.
Love and Happy Birthday.
Uncle Bill.

Mum looked at the word *zough* and frowned. 'Bill can't spell for nuts,' she said. 'I think he meant *tough* or maybe *rough.*'

'That doesn't make sense,' I said.

'Bill never makes sense,' said Mum. 'Fancy giving you a dead rat for your birthday.'

The rat stood there stiff and still inside a little glass dome. Its mouth was open in a sort of a snarl.

'It's cute,' I said. 'Uncle Bill always gives me great presents.'

Mum gave a snort. 'Bill's up in Darwin getting into all sorts of foolishness. He knows we're dead broke. And what does he give you? Shoes? Books? A new school uniform? Something useful? Not on your Nelly. He gives you a stuffed rat, for heaven's sake.'

'I like him,' I said.

'I like him too,' said Mum. 'But I'm glad he's in Darwin and we're down here in Melbourne. Fancy giving you a dead rat. He probably got it for nothing.'

I could understand why Mum wanted me to have clothes for my birthday. Life was tough for her. She had been working hard. Too hard. She needed a holiday and I was trying to arrange it. All I had to do was get three thousand dollars for the two of us to go to Surfers Paradise. I had been saving for two weeks and already had one dollar fifty. Only two thousand, nine hundred and ninety-eight dollars fifty to go.

When Uncle Bill made it big he was going to send us money. But at the moment he was broke too. Mum sometimes called her brother 'Silly Billy'. But I liked him. He was always having adventures.

I read the letter again. 'The Spitting Rat brings good luck if you take it to a zough,' I said.

'I wouldn't get your hopes up, dear,' said Mum.

'I'll test it out,' I said. 'Maybe the luck works without a zough – whatever that is.' I went over to the cupboard and fetched two dice from a game of Ludo. Then I shook them up and threw them on the table.

'Two sixes,' I yelled.

'A fluke,' said Mum with a laugh. She walked out of the kitchen, shaking her head and not even waiting to see what happened.

I threw the dice again and stared. I couldn't believe it. Another two sixes.

The stuffed rat glared out from its glass cage. Was it bringing me luck? I threw the dice once more. They both rolled off the edge of the table and under the sideboard that Uncle Bill gave me last year. I couldn't see if they had thrown up sixes or not. I lay down on my stomach and peered into the dusty space where the dice had stopped. There was something there. A piece of paper sticking out of my cupboard.

I reached under and pulled the dice and the paper out. It wasn't just any old piece of paper. It was a fifty dollar note.

'Wow,' I screamed. 'Bonus. What luck.'

Just for fun I threw the dice again. Two sixes. Yes, yes, yes. The rat was a lucky rat, that was for sure.

I showed Mum the money. 'If the Spitting Rat had not arrived we would never have found this fifty dollars,' I said. 'It brings luck. Now we only have to find another $2,948.50 and we can have that holiday up north in the sun.'

Mum gave me a kindly smile. 'It's a lovely thing you are doing, Anthony,' she said. 'But three thousand dollars is too much for a boy to save all on his own. I'd be just as happy if you did the washing-up now and then.'

Poor Mum. Fancy thinking that me doing the washing-up was going to make her happy. No – I had to get the three thousand dollars. Then she could relax next to a pool in Surfers Paradise. And neither of us would have to do the washing-up.

I sat down and wrote a letter back to Uncle Bill.

Dear Uncle Bill,
Thanks for the Spitting Rat. It is grate. By the way, what's a zough?
I am going in a speling compatition today. The prize is a free trip to Surfers Paradice. If I win I am going to take Mum. She needs a rest.
Lots of love,
Anthony.

The spelling competition was on that very day. At five o'clock in the town hall.

'I'm pretty good at spelling,' I said to Mum. 'I might win the competition.'

Mum read my letter and smiled. 'You're so much like Bill,' she said with a smile.

I could see she didn't think much of my chances. I don't know why. I was a good speller. Still, I had to have a fall-back plan. An idea started to form in my mind. Yes. It was a good idea. I would use money to make money. Invest it wisely.

I put the fifty dollars and the two dice into my pocket and picked up the rat's dome. 'I'm going out for a while,' I told Mum. 'I'll be back soon.'

2

We lived on the top floor of the high-rise commission flats. I made my way to the lift and pressed the button for the ground floor. The lift was covered in graffiti and the wall was covered in spit. I hated the look of spit. Yuck.

I stepped out of the lift and made my way to the nearest newsagency. I tucked the rat under my arm and held the glass cage tightly. I wanted to give the rat every chance of passing the good luck on to me.

'One five dollar scratchy, please, Mrs Filby,' I said.

Mrs Filby shook her head. 'You have to be over fifteen to buy Lotto tickets, Anthony,' she said.

'It's for Mum,' I said.

It wasn't really a lie. It was for Mum's holiday up north. That's what I told myself anyway.

Mrs Filby wasn't sure but she took the five dollars and gave me the scratch lottery ticket.

I walked over to the little-kids' playground and sat inside a painted drainpipe with the Spitting Rat and my scratch ticket.

You had to get three numbers the same to win that amount of money. There were four different panels to scratch away and reveal the amounts of money.

I uncovered the first panel. $10,000, $25, $15, $10,000 and . . . wait for it, wait for it, stay calm. Oh, rats. $10. Jeez, that was close.

I almost won ten thousand dollars.

I tried the next group. $100,000, $250,000, $250,000, and, and, and . . . $250,000. Yahoo. I had won. Three lots of two hundred and fifty thousand dollars. Awesome. Magic. My heart was pumping like crazy.

Hang on, hang on. Oh no. One of them was twenty-five thousand not two hundred and fifty thousand. I felt like someone who was on the end of the queue just as McDonald's closed for the day. No hamburger. Nothing.

I quickly uncovered the third panel. No luck. Rats.

One last window to go. Scratch, scratch, scratch. I did them all quickly without really looking. And then I saw it. Oh, yes. Three lots of three thousand dollars. There was no mistake. I blinked and blinked and pinched myself. I had won three thousand dollars.

The Spitting Rat was the lucky rat. That was for sure. I jumped up and banged my head on the top of the concrete pipe.

'Ow, wow, arghoo.' It hurt like crazy. I fell down backwards and smashed into the glass dome of the Spitting Rat. And broke it. It just smashed to pieces leaving the rat standing in the not so fresh air.

What had I done? Would the rat still bring luck? Would it get mad at me?

'Sorry, Ratty,' I said. 'I'm really sorry.'

I patted the still, stuffed rat on its head. As if to make it feel better.

3

That's when it happened. Right when I touched the rat. That's when all my troubles started. I still can't believe that it actually happened, but it did.

The rat took a quick, sharp breath. I heard it quite clearly.

My mouth fell open in surprise.

And the rat spat.

Yes, the dead rat spat. Right into my mouth.

Oh, yucko. Gross. Foul. Disgusting. I could feel the rat's spit on my tongue. Hot, sizzling, terrible.

I tried to spit it out but I couldn't. Something took hold of my mouth muscles and I swallowed the rat spit right down into my stomach.

The rat just stood there as if nothing had happened. Silent, stiff and dead as a stone. Its beady eyes stared ahead as if they were made of glass. What am I talking about? They *were* made of glass.

I shook my head in disbelief. Maybe it was a dream. A day-dream. Maybe I had just imagined that the rat spat.

Anyway, it didn't really matter. I still had my Lotto ticket. A three thousand dollar payout was heading my way. And Mum and I were heading for the sunshine. I was stoked. Now it wouldn't matter if I won or lost the spelling competition. I had my three thousand dollars *and* the forty-five dollars change from the fifty.

I picked up the rat and headed back to collect my prize.

As I crossed the street a kid came whizzing past me on a bike. It was Michael Smeds, a boy I knew from school. Suddenly I drew a breath. A sharp little intake of air. My mouth just seemed to have a mind of its own. I didn't want to take that breath. I had no choice.

And I had no choice in what happened next.

I spat.

A little blue bit of spit (yes, blue – and hot) went shooting through the air and hit the front tyre of the bike. Smeds lost control, started to wobble and crashed into a lamp-post. I went over and helped him up. He wasn't hurt but his front wheel was buckled. And it had a flat tyre.

'You spat at me,' he yelled. 'It made me fall. What did you do that for? I'll get you for that. Just you wait.' He started to wheel his bike along the footpath, heading angrily for home.

'I'm sorry,' I called out. 'I didn't mean to have a go at you.'

The whole thing was crazy. Hot, blue spit. I must have caught some terrible disease from the rat. I needed help. But not before I collected my three thousand smackeroos.

I walked onto the Yarra River footbridge and looked down into the brown water. It was so peaceful. A bloke and his girlfriend were just passing under me in a small rowing boat.

Suddenly I took a quick breath. I tried to keep my mouth closed. I gritted my teeth. I breathed in through my nose. But it was no good. I lost the struggle. *Phshst* . . . A hot, blue gob of spit dropped down towards the boat. *Splot.* It landed right in the middle near the girl's feet.

4

In a flash a little stream of water began to squirt up inside the boat. It grew stronger and bigger. After a few seconds it was like a broken fire hydrant flooding up into the sky. And then, before I could blink, the boat was gone. Sunk. Sent to the bottom of the Yarra.

The two rowers started to swim for the bank. The man

looked up angrily at me and yelled out something. They were good swimmers. They looked fit and strong. They looked as if they could tear a thirteen-year-old kid into pieces without much trouble.

I turned and ran for it. I just belted along without knowing where I was going. Finally I fell panting and exhausted under a bush in the Fitzroy Gardens.

I dumped the Spitting Rat down and tried to gather my thoughts.

This was dangerous. I had spat at a bike and punctured it. I had spat at a boat and sunk it. I never knew when I was going to spit next. It was out of my control.

I had to get away from the rat. Maybe if I put some distance between me and it I would be cured. Maybe its powers wouldn't work at a distance. I shoved the rat under a bush and headed for home.

I was really worried. Even the thought of the winning lottery ticket didn't make any difference. I had to spit when I didn't want to. It was hot and blue and yucky and burned holes into things.

As I walked I started to imagine things. The spit was powerful. Maybe if the Australian Army found out about it they could use the spit as a weapon. They could bottle it and throw it like hand grenades at the enemy. But the spit was powerful stuff. It would probably eat through the bottles.

Maybe the army would put me in the front line. I would have to spit at the enemy tanks as they came along the road. No thanks. No way.

I hurried back to the commission flats and jumped into the lift. I pressed the button for the twentieth floor. The doors banged shut and I started to go up. I was alone in the lift.

The floors whizzed by. Seventeen, eighteen, nineteen. Suddenly I took a quick breath. Don't spit. Don't, don't, don't. I put one hand on top of my head and the other under my jaw. I pushed as hard as I could, trying, trying, trying to keep my mouth shut.

My mouth suddenly exploded. I just couldn't stop it. *Kersplot.* A bright-blue bit of spittle sizzled on the floor. Like an egg in a frying-pan it spat and crackled. Suddenly a small hole opened in the lift floor and the spit disappeared.

I could see right down to the bottom of the lift-well. Long cables clanked and clanged. My head started to swim and I felt sick. What if my spit had landed on a cable and eaten through it? I could have fallen to my death.

I was a long way from the Spitting Rat. It didn't seem to make any difference. I was still cursed with its spiteful, spitting spell.

5

I hurried out of the lift and ran to our flat. Mum wasn't home but I wasn't taking any chances. I banged my bedroom door shut and locked it. I needed time to think. A terrible thought was growing somewhere deep inside and I didn't want to let it out.

I tried to figure it out. The blue spit could eat through anything. And I didn't know when it was going to happen. I couldn't stop spitting no matter how hard I tried.

But. And it was a big but. Would the spit have its terrible powers if I tried it on purpose?

I looked around for something I didn't need. A piece of rock that I used to keep the door open. I placed it on the floor. Then I worked up a bit of spit in my mouth and let fly.

Yes. It settled on the rock and began to fizz, bright and blue. In no time at all the rock had gone altogether. There was just a little blue smear left on the floor.

Suddenly I started to suck in – *kersploosh.* Another small blue bomb landed on my spelling book. It started to fizz and disappeared.

I was taken with a spitting frenzy. I spat on everything. My skateboard vanished in a fizzing blue mess. And my photo of Mum. Everything was a target. My bed was riddled with bubbling holes. My desk was drilled right through. The light-shade vanished. My football collapsed with a bang.

Breathe, spit. Breathe, spit. Breathe, spit. I couldn't stop myself. I was out of control.

Finally I fell to the floor exhausted. The spitting spasm had finished.

For now.

I heard the front door slam. Mum was home.

Mum.

Now the terrible thought managed to surface. I had to face it. What if I spat at Mum? Oh, horrible thought. No, no, no.

I was dangerous. I was a menace to society. Everything

I spat at was destroyed. I could kill people.

There was only one thing to do. I had to go away from human beings. Hide deep in the forest. Or find a deserted island. I would never see a person again. I couldn't even have a dog because I might be seized with a spitting fit and accidentally kill it.

Such was the power of the terrible Spitting Rat. A sad and lonely future stretched before me and I was only a kid.

And what about Mum? What would she do without me? She wouldn't have anyone to cook for. No one's bed to make. No one to eat her cakes.

The door-handle suddenly rattled. 'Are you in there, Anthony?' said Mum's voice. 'What are you doing? Playing with that rat, I suppose.'

'I threw it out,' I yelled through the door.

There was a long silence. 'Sometimes I could murder Bill,' said Mum. 'What was he thinking of? Giving you a dead rat for your birthday.'

Her voice trailed off and I could hear her banging around in the kitchen. She always did the washing-up when she was angry. It made her feel better. She was a good mother. I had to get away before I hurt her.

I took out a pencil and started to write a note. My last message to my mum.

Dear Mum,

I love you very much. For the safty of the world I have to go away and be on my own. Do not try to find me or your life will be in danjer. Here is a winning lotery ticket. I want you to have that hollerday up north in the sun.

Your loving son,

Anthony.

I folded up my letter and took out the lottery ticket.

I could feel it coming. Sort of building up inside me. Don't let it. Don't, don't, don't. Too late. I snatched a breath and spat. Right on the Lotto ticket. It fizzled for a second and was gone. Disappeared. Totally destroyed.

I hung my head on the drilled-out desk and let a tear run down my nose.

Now Mum would never get to Queensland.

Why had Uncle Bill given me that rat? He had let us down. Put my life in danger. Still and all – he did tell me not to touch the rat. It wasn't really his fault.

Anger started to boil inside me. My life was ruined. My money was gone. All because of . . . Not Uncle Bill – no, not him. I wasn't mad at him. It was all the Spitting Rat's fault.

The rage inside me made me think. There was a way I could pay it back. There was a way I could get even. I would get my revenge on the rat.

I ran out of my room and out of the flat before Mum could say a word. Along the corridor to the lift. No way. Down the fire escape – the lift was too risky.

Across the playground. Over the bridge. Up to the bush in the Fitzroy Gardens.

It was time for the rat to get a bit of its own medicine.

6

I found two sticks and lifted the Spitting Rat out of the bushes by holding one on each side of its neck. I was careful not to touch it.

'Now,' I yelled. 'You've ruined my life. But you're not getting off free.'

I snatched a breath. And spat. Straight at the face of the Spitting Rat. A little blue gob of spit sped at its victim like a bullet.

But the rat was too quick. Without warning it opened its mouth. Fast like a dog snapping at a fly. Slurp. Swallow. The spit was gone. The rat had taken it back.

Straight away the rat went back to normal. It stood there. Stuffed, still and slightly silly. Just as if nothing had happened.

And I went back to normal too. My mouth felt different. I worked up a bit of moisture and spat on the ground. Normal, clear spit. No spitting and fizzing.

'OK, Mr Ratty,' I said. 'So I'm cured. But what about my luck? Are you still lucky for me?'

I took out the two dice and rolled them. A five and a two.

The luck was gone. No more blue spit and no more money.

I pushed the rat back under the bushes with the sticks and walked sadly home. Now my only hope was to win the spelling competition. Two free tickets to Queensland for the winner.

I looked at my watch. I just had time to make it to the town hall.

7

There were hundreds of kids in the town hall. We were all sitting at desks that had big spaces between them so that no one could cheat.

'Pick up your pens,' said the Spelling Master.

The hall was filled with the sound of two hundred pens being lifted at the same time.

I crossed my fingers and hoped for luck. I hoped the words would not be too hard.

'The gangster fired a bullet. Spell *bullet,*' said the Spelling Master.

'Easy,' I lied to myself. I wrote each letter carefully. B-u-l-l-i-t.

'I went *through* the door. Spell *through,*' said the Spelling Master.

Oh no. This was a tough one. How did you spell through? T-h-r-e-w? Nah. T-h-r-o-o? No way. I couldn't get it. I just couldn't work it out. My head was spinning. Everything was going wrong. I had another try. I slowly wrote down the letters and stared at them. T-h-r-o-u-g-h. That was it. Yes, *ough* says *oo*. Like in *zoo*. I scratched my head and wondered.

'Aghh,' I suddenly screamed at the top of my voice. I flung my pencil on the floor and ran out of the door. Everyone stared. They thought I was crazy.

8
THREE WEEKS LATER

'Last call for Qantas Flight QF 628 to Brisbane,' said the announcer's voice at the airport. 'This flight closes at 3.50 p.m.'

'Come on,' I said to Mum. 'Let's go.' We hurried onto the plane. Outside the Melbourne rain was falling softly on the runway. 'Sunshine, here we come,' I said.

Mum headed down towards the back of the plane.

'Not that way,' I said. 'These are First Class tickets.'

We sat down among the business people wearing suits and balancing computer notebooks on their knees. The flight attendant brought us fresh orange juice.

Mum was really curious. 'Come on, Anthony,' she said with a smile. 'I know you couldn't have won the spelling competition. You're no better at spelling than Uncle Bill. So where did you get the money?'

I grinned. 'Spitting Rats are extinct,' I said. 'There are none left alive. A man from the zoo gave me three thousand dollars for it. Just the right amount.'

'The zoo?' said Mum. 'Why the zoo?'

I took out the little notepad that they give you in First Class and wrote a word.

'*Zough* rhymes with *zoo*,' I said. 'Like *through*. Uncle Bill wanted me to take the rat to the zoo. He knew it would bring us luck.'

Mum gave the biggest smile ever. She was so happy to be going on a holiday.

'I like Bill,' she said. 'But he's a bit nutty. I'm glad he lives over two thousand k's away.'

The plane started to speed along the runway.

'Yahoo,' I yelled.

'Where are we going anyway?' Mum said. 'You can't keep it secret any longer.'

The plane lifted into the air. 'Brisbane first,' I said. 'Then on to Darwin to see Uncle Bill.'

Mum started to laugh like crazy. It was good to see.

Jack Dillon

from Survive! Volcanic Fury

1

Sam Carlsen heard a rumbling sound, coming from somewhere above, and felt a faint shuddering under his feet. He looked up to where he could just see the grey crags rising to the volcano's cone. Plumes of smoke were rising high into the air, but there was no sign of anything that could have made the noise.

Jo was looking up as well. 'Did you hear that?'

'What was it?' Mike asked.

Sam shrugged. 'Dunno. Thunder, maybe.'

He knew as he spoke how stupid that was. There wasn't a cloud in the sky.

Jo jumped from the last stone to the bank at his side and said, 'I thought at first it might be somebody looking for us. Another helicopter. But it didn't sound like an engine.'

'Maybe volcanoes make funny noises.'

Russ joined them on the far bank of the stream. He said nothing about the noise, and Sam didn't want to go on talking about it in case Mike got even more scared.

'Listen,' Russ said. 'I've been thinking. The helicopter must be leaking fuel. It could catch fire or even blow up. Let me go up there first and check it out. You wait here.'

Without waiting for a reply, he set off up the slope, using his hands to pull himself up the steeper parts. Sam watched him go. Jo and Mike squatted on the bank.

The rumbling sound came again. This time it grew louder, swelling to a roar. Halfway up the slope, Russ straightened. Then he spun round. 'Sam!' he yelled. 'Everybody! Get up here! Fast!'

Skidding, half falling, he scrambled back towards them. Sam stared upwards. Along the gully, where the stream had flowed peacefully among the stones, a huge wall of mud exploded into sight. Branches were being tossed around in it; foam frothed brown against the sky. The air was suddenly heavy with the reek of sulphur.

Sam stood, frozen, as the flood bore down towards him.

2

'Sam! Snap out of it!' Russ yelled. He grabbed Sam's arm and thrust him towards the slope. 'Up! Jo, Mike, get up here! Fast!'

Sam saw Jo push Mike upwards and his father gave the younger boy a hand. He came out of his momentary shock. Grabbing frantically at stones and plant stems, he forced himself to climb, faster and faster as the mud swept with a thundering roar down the gully, filling it.

He saw mud rush past his feet and knew he had not escaped yet. The level was rising all the time. He needed to get higher – away from the churning brown ooze. Breath sobbing, arms and legs aching, he hauled himself away from the engulfing mud.

Behind him, a scream cut through the roar of the flood. Sam glanced round. His dad and Mike were level with him; just below, Jo had lost her footing on the edge of the mud. As it surged over her, Sam saw her grab at a clump of overhanging leaves, but they gave way under her weight. She screamed again as the mud swept her away.

Mike shouted, 'Jo! Jo!' and started to climb down towards her.

Russ snapped at him, 'No, stay here. Sam, keep him out of this.' He shoved his camera bag into Sam's arms and flung himself down the slope, sliding on a diagonal, trying to intercept Jo further down.

Sam dumped the bag. Whatever his dad said, he couldn't just stand and watch. 'Come on,' he said to Mike.

He started to scramble crab-wise across the slope, trying to stay above the mud but stay abreast of his dad and Jo further down. The level had stopped rising, he thought, or at least it was rising very slowly now, and the terrifying thunder was dying away into a low, rushing noise.

Jo was still in sight, her face a white blob against the mud, one arm free and waving wildly, but the torrent was sweeping her down too fast for Russ to catch her.

'She'll sink!' Mike screamed.

Panting, Sam said, 'Keep going.'

'It's no good! We can't do anything.'

A curve in the gully took Jo out of sight. A moment later, Russ disappeared over the shoulder of the hill.

'Cut across!' Sam yelled to Mike. 'We might catch her further down.'

He laboured up to the top of the rise and stood there, panting. Just below, the slope grew steeper still and then it levelled out until it disappeared under the surface of the mud flow. Russ was squatting down on the edge.

'Where's Jo?' Mike gasped.

Sam thought he heard a faint cry, but he wasn't sure where it came from. He slid down towards his father. The mud flow was running more slowly now, the surface churning like soup. As Sam drew closer, he saw Jo, a few metres upstream of Russ, being carried down to where he was waiting. Only her head and one arm were visible; her face and hair were plastered with mud, as if her head had gone under, but she was still alive.

Sam let out a cry of relief. 'Mike, she's here!'

Russ was reaching out to her. Jo strained to catch hold of his hand, but Sam could see that she was going to be swept past.

'Help! I can't reach!' she cried.

As she came level with him, Russ floundered a few paces into the mud and caught hold of her outstretched arm. For a few seconds they clung together; the mud came up to Russ's chest, and Sam could see that he was going to be carried off his feet.

'Dad!' he yelled.

Sam skidded to a stop at the edge of the mud flow. Mike was panting just behind him. Sam gazed wildly around and caught sight of a scrawny bush growing a metre or so away from the edge. 'Mike! Grab hold of that!'

Mike saw what he meant. He grasped one of the branches and held his other hand out to Sam. They gripped each other's wrists, and Sam stepped cautiously out into the mud.

He could feel the suction as he edged out to where his father was still fighting to keep his balance and hang on to Jo at the same time. Russ grinned and held out a hand. 'Great, Sam,' he said. 'Just take it slowly.'

Sam waded out another couple of steps. The mud was up to his knees. His arms and Mike's were at full stretch now. 'Mike, don't let go!' he warned.

Then he felt his dad's fingers fasten round his wrist. There was a sudden wrench as Sam took the extra weight.

'OK,' Russ said. 'Pull us in. Steady.'

At first Sam thought he couldn't move. The mud was pushing against him, wanting to tear him away from his grip on Mike. He forced himself to take a step back towards the bank. Then another. He could hear his breath coming in rapid gasps. Another step back. He was almost clear of the stuff by now, and the level had sunk to his dad's waist.

Russ had an arm round Jo, keeping her head and shoulders clear of the mud. She managed a weak grin, and said, 'Go, Sam.'

Mike cried out, 'Sam, the branch!'

Not looking, Sam made one massive effort and threw himself backwards. He felt his dad release him. With a horrible sucking sound the mud let him go; he stumbled on to solid ground and lost his grip on Mike as he fell to his knees. Jo had found her feet; she and Russ floundered back to the edge together and collapsed, side by side, on the bank. Sam glanced back at Mike; the younger boy was standing beside the bush, staring at the branch that had come away in his hands.

Russ was sitting with his head in his hands. Jo lay, face down, her body heaving as she took in deep gulps of air.

'Jo!' Mike said, kneeling beside her. 'Jo, are you all right?'

After a minute, his sister rolled over and reached out to give his arm a shake. 'No, I'm not. I'm filthy and exhausted and I've swallowed about a gallon of that stuff.'

Mike suddenly grinned widely. 'She's OK!'

Jo sat up and rubbed her hands over her face and hair, shaking off great clots of mud. 'I said I wanted a wash, not a mud bath.' Serious suddenly, she added, 'Thanks. All of you.'

Sam just felt relieved that she was safe. There was more to Jo than he'd thought at first. She really had guts; if nothing else, the crisis had shown him that.

'What I don't understand,' he said, 'is where all that mud came from. It hasn't rained for ages.'

'Well . . . there's only one place where we've seen that much water,' said Russ.

'The crater lake?'

His dad nodded. 'If the crater wall collapsed, the

water would rush out and pick up soil and rock on its way. It's a well-known volcanic phenomenon,' he added. 'They call it a lahar.'

'Mr Carlsen,' Jo said in a dead-pan voice, 'you've no idea how much better I feel, knowing that.'

'Then what made the crater wall collapse?' Mike asked. 'Is the volcano going to erupt?'

Sam spun round and stared up at the cone, but it remained grey and silent, still wreathed in smoke. He had always thought that volcanic eruptions meant ash and molten lava, not mud. Tangaroa showed no signs of producing those. At least, not yet, he thought to himself.

'I don't know,' said Russ, in reply to Mike's question. 'But if there is going to be trouble, then the best we can do is get back to the helicopter and send off a distress call.'

Evacuation!

If you lived close to an active volcano that was expected to erupt, you would have to be prepared to evacuate your home at short notice. You may have to travel on foot, by car or by truck or even by ship in coastal areas.

DO NOT argue with the authorities if you are told to leave your home. It is for your own safety. In most places you would face a fine if you were to enter a forbidden zone near an active volcano.

DO stay calm.

DO NOT guess where you need to go. The experts can predict with some accuracy which areas are most likely to be affected.

DO find out exactly where the safe havens are located. Emergency shelters are often set up in schools and community halls.

DO leave everything behind that you don't need.

DO NOT stay around to watch the spectacle. It may be an incredible sight, but the consequences are not worth the risk.

Volcanoes – The Facts

What?
A volcano is a mountain or hill that contains one or more openings in the earth's crust through which lava, cinders, steam, gases and other matter are forcefully ejected – continuously or at intervals.

Where?
Volcanoes are likely to occur wherever one or more of the earth's continental plates meet. Most active is The Ring of Fire – roughly the area surrounding the Pacific Ocean. Major volcanoes are also found in the mid-Atlantic Ocean, in the West Indies, the Hawaiian islands, the Mediterranean and Indonesia.

When?
Volcanic activity is extremely unpredictable. Earth tremors, increased temperatures and minor eruptions can all indicate rising activity. However, even with modern technology, only rarely will sufficient warning be given to prepare fully for a major eruption.

How?
Volcanoes begin as hot spots – molten magma builds up in huge chambers deep underneath the earth's crust. Under great pressure, the magma begins to move towards the surface through fissures. When the crust is eventually punctured, a volcanic eruption occurs and continues until the pressure underground subsides. Eruptions can also be triggered by the escape of gases or by the side of a volcano collapsing.

Dick King-Smith

Fat Lawrence

Cats come in roughly three sizes – skinny, middling or fat. There is a fourth size – very fat.

But seldom do you see such a one as Lawrence Higgins. Lawrence was a cat of a fifth size – very, very fat indeed. He was black, and so big and heavy that his owner, Mrs Higgins of Rosevale, Forest Street, Morchester, could not lift him even an inch from the ground.

'Oh, Lawrence Higgins!' she would say (she had named the cat after her late husband, even though he had actually been quite small and thin). 'Oh, Lawrence Higgins! Why are you so fat? It isn't as though I overfeed you. You only get one meal a day.'

And this was true. At around eight o'clock in the morning Lawrence would come into Rosevale through the cat flap, from wherever he'd been since the previous day, to receive his breakfast.

Then, when he had eaten the bowl of cat-meat which Mrs Higgins put before him, he would hoist his black bulk into an armchair and sleep till midday. Then out he would go again, where to Mrs Higgins never knew. She had become used to the fact that her cat only ever spent the mornings at Rosevale.

Five doors further down Forest Street, at Hillview, Mr and Mrs Norman also had a cat, a black cat, the fattest black cat you ever saw.

'Oh, Lawrence Norman!' Mrs Norman would say (they knew his name was Lawrence, they'd read it on a disc attached to his collar, that day, months ago now, when he had suddenly appeared on their window sill, mewing – at lunchtime, it was). 'Oh, Lawrence Norman! Why are you so fat?'

'It isn't as though you overfeed him,' said Mr Norman.

'No,' said his wife. 'He only gets one meal a day.'

And this was true. At lunchtime Mrs Norman would hear Lawrence mewing and let him in and give him a bowl of cat-meat.

Then, when he had eaten it, he would heave his black bulk on to the sofa and sleep till teatime. Then off he would go again, the Normans never knew where. They'd become accustomed to the fact that their cat only spent the afternoon at Hillview.

Round the corner, in the next street, Woodland Way, there lived at Number 33 an old man called Mr Mason, alone save for his enormously fat black cat. It had slipped in through his back door one day months ago – at teatime it was – and he had read its name on its collar.

'Oh, Lawrence Mason!' he would say as, hearing that scratch on the back door, he let the black cat in, and put down a bowl of cat-meat. 'Oh, Lawrence Mason! Why are you so fat? It isn't as if I overfeed you. I only give you this one meal a day and that's the truth.'

When Lawrence Mason had emptied the bowl, he would stretch his black bulk out on the hearth rug and sleep till suppertime. Then out he would go again, where to old Mr Mason did not know. All he knew was that his cat only spent the evening at Number 33.

In front of Woodland Way was the Park, and on the other side of the Park the houses were larger and posher. In one of them, The Gables, Pevensey Place, lived Colonel and Mrs Barclay-Lloyd and their cat, who had arrived one evening at suppertime, months ago now, wearing a collar with his name on it.

Mrs Barclay-Lloyd had opened the front door of The Gables, and there, sitting at the top of the flight of steps that led up from the street, was this enormously fat black cat.

Each evening now at suppertime the Barclay-Lloyds would set before Lawrence a dish of chicken nuggets and a saucer of Gold Top milk.

'Lawrence Barclay-Lloyd!' the Colonel would say. 'I cannot understand why you are so fat.'

'To look at him,' his wife would say, 'anyone would think he was getting four meals a day instead of just the one that we give him.'

When Lawrence had eaten his chicken and drunk his milk, he would hump his black bulk up the stairs, and clamber on to the foot of the Barclay-Lloyds' four-poster bed, and fall fast asleep.

The Colonel and his wife took to going to bed early too, knowing that at around seven o'clock next morning they would be woken by their cat mewing loudly to be let out of The Gables. They never knew where he went, only that they would not see him again until the following evening.

For a long while Lawrence was not only the fattest but also the happiest cat you can imagine. Assured of comfortable places to sleep and the certainty of four good square meals a day, he had not a care in the world.

But gradually, as time went on and he grew, would you believe it, even fatter, he began to feel that all this travelling – from Rosevale to Hillview, from Hillview to Number 33, from Number 33 to The Gables, and then back from The Gables all the way to Rosevale – was too much of a good thing. All that walking, now that his black bulk was so vast, was tiring. In addition, he suffered from indigestion.

One summer evening while making his way from Woodland Way to Pevensey Place for supper, he stopped at the edge of a small boating-lake in the middle of the Park.

As he bent his head to lap, he caught sight of his reflection in the water.

'Lawrence, my boy,' he said. 'You are carrying too much weight. You'd better do something about it. But what? I'll see what the boys say.'

The 'boys' were Lawrence's four particular friends. Each lived near one of his addresses.

Opposite Rosevale, on the other side of Forest Street, Fernmount was the home of a ginger tom called Bert, who of course knew the black cat as Lawrence Higgins. Next day after breakfast, Lawrence paid a call on him.

'Bert,' he said. 'D'you think I'm carrying too much weight?'

'If you carry much more, Higgins, old pal,' said Bert, 'you'll break your blooming back. Mrs Higgins must feed you well.'

'She only gives me one meal a day,' Lawrence said.

After lunch, he visited the second of the boys, who also lived in Forest Street, at Restholm, a couple of doors beyond Hillview. He was a tabby tom named Fred, who of course knew the black cat as Lawrence Norman.

'Fred,' said Lawrence. 'Tell me straight, tom to tom. Would you call me fat?'

'Norman, old chum,' said Fred. 'You are as fat as a pig. The Normans must shovel food into you.'

'They only give me one meal a day,' said Lawrence.

After tea he waddled round the corner into Woodland Way, where at Number 35 there lived a white tom called Percy. He of course knew the black cat as Lawrence Mason.

'Percy,' said Lawrence. 'Give me some advice . . .'

Percy, like many white cats, was rather deaf.

'Give you some of my mice?' he said. 'Not likely, Mason, old mate, you don't need any extra food, anyone can see that. You eat too much already.'

'Do you think I should go on a diet?' asked Lawrence.

'Do I think you're going to die of it?' said Percy. 'Yes, probably. Old Mason must be stuffing food into you.'

'He only gives me one meal a day,' said Lawrence loudly.

Percy heard this.

'One meal a week, Mason,' he said. 'That's all you need.'

Later, Lawrence plodded across the Park (being careful not to look at his reflection in the boating-lake), and in Pevensey Place he called in at The Cedars, which was opposite The Gables. Here lived the fourth of the boys, a Blue Persian tom by the name of Darius.

Darius was not only extremely handsome, with his small wide-set ears and his big round eyes and his snub nose and his long flowing blue coat. He was also much more intelligent than Bert or Fred or Percy.

'What's up, Barclay-Lloyd, old boy?' he said when he saw Lawrence. 'You're puffing and blowing like a grampus. You're going to have to do something about yourself, you know.'

'The Colonel and his wife only feed me once a day,' said Lawrence.

'I dare say,' replied Darius. 'But look here, Barclay-Lloyd, old boy, I wasn't born yesterday, you know. You're getting more than one meal a day, aren't you now?'

'Yes,' said Lawrence.

'How many?'

'Four altogether.'

'So at three other houses besides The Gables?'

'Yes.'

'Bad show, Barclay-Lloyd,' said Darius. 'You'll have to cut down. If you don't, then in my opinion you're going to eat yourself to death. Just think how much better you'll feel if you lose some of that weight. You won't get so puffed, you'll be leaner and fitter, and your girlfriend will find you much more attractive.'

'I haven't got a girlfriend, Darius,' said Lawrence sadly.

'And why is that, Barclay-Lloyd, old boy?' said Darius. 'Ask yourself why.'

'Because I'm too fat?'

'Undoubtedly.'

'A figure of fun, would you say?'

'Afraid so.'

'Actually, girls do tend to giggle at me.'

'Not surprised.'

Lawrence took a deep breath. 'All right,' he said. 'I'll do it, Darius. I'll go on a diet.'

'Good show, Barclay-Lloyd,' said Darius.

'I'll cut down to three meals a day,' said Lawrence.

'One.'

'Two?'

'One,' said Darius firmly. 'One good meal a day is all any cat needs.'

For a little while Lawrence sat, thinking.

Then he said, 'But if I'm only to have one meal a day, I only need to go to one house.'

'What's wrong with The Gables?' said Darius.

'Nothing,' said Lawrence. 'They give me chicken nuggets and Gold Top milk.'

'What!' said Darius. 'Well, you can cut the milk out, for a start. Water for you from now on, old boy.'

'But if I just stay here,' said Lawrence, 'the other people will be worried. They'll wonder where I've got to – Mrs Higgins and the Normans and old Mr Mason. And I shan't see the other boys – Bert and Fred and Percy.'

For a little while Darius sat, thinking.

Then he said, 'There are two ways to play this, Barclay-Lloyd. One is – you continue to make the rounds of your houses, but in each you only eat a quarter of what they put before you. Then that'll add up to one meal a day. Are you strong-minded enough to leave three-quarters of a bowlful at each meal?'

'No,' said Lawrence.

'Then,' said Darius, 'the only thing to do is for you to spend the whole day at each house, in turn. And if you take my advice, you'll cut out breakfast, lunch and tea. Stick to supper. Which reminds me, it's time for mine. Cheerio, Barclay-Lloyd, old boy, and the best of luck with your diet.'

To the surprise of the Colonel and his wife, that Sunday evening Lawrence didn't touch his milk. He ate the chicken, certainly, greedily in fact, as though it was his last meal for some time, and he went to sleep on the foot of the four-poster as usual. But the next morning no mewing roused the Barclay-Lloyds, and when they did wake, it was to find Lawrence still with them and apparently in no hurry to move.

On Monday, breakfast time came and went with no sign of Lawrence Higgins at Rosevale.

Lunchtime in Hillview passed without Lawrence Norman.

At Number 33 Lawrence Mason did not appear for tea.

Old Mr Mason was worried about his black cat, as were the Normans. So was Mrs Higgins, but her worry ceased as Lawrence popped in through the cat flap at Rosevale that evening.

'Lawrence Higgins!' she cried. 'Where *have* you been? You must be starving.'

Lawrence would have agreed, could he have understood her words, and he polished off the bowl of cat-meat that was put before him and hoisted his black bulk into the armchair, and, much to Mrs Higgins' surprise, spent the night there.

On Tuesday evening Lawrence Norman appeared for supper at Hillview.

On Wednesday evening Lawrence Mason ate at Number 33.

Not until the Thursday evening did Lawrence Barclay-Lloyd reappear for supper at The Gables, much to the relief of the Colonel and his wife, who of course had not set eyes on their black cat since Sunday.

Gradually everyone grew used to this strange new state of affairs – that their black cat now only turned up every four days.

And gradually, as the weeks passed, Lawrence grew thinner.

The boys noticed this (though only one of them knew why).

'You on a diet, Higgins, old pal?' asked Bert.

'Sort of,' said Lawrence.

'You're looking a lot fitter, Norman, old chum,' said Fred.

'I feel it,' said Lawrence.

To Percy he said, 'I've lost some weight.'

'What's that, Mason, old mate?' said Percy.

'I've lost some weight.'

'Lost your plate?' said Percy.

'No, weight.'

'Eh?'

'*Weight!*' shouted Lawrence.

'Why should I?' said Percy. 'What am I meant to be waiting for?'

As for Darius, he was delighted that his plan for his friend was working so well.

After months of dieting, Lawrence was positively slim.

'Jolly good show, Barclay-Lloyd, old boy,' purred the Persian. 'The girls will never be able to resist you.'

'I don't know any.'

'Well, between you and me and the gatepost,' said Darius, 'there's a little cracker living down at the other end of Pevensey Place. Tortoiseshell-and-white, she is. Dream of a figure. Amazing orange eyes. You'd make a grand pair.'

So next morning Lawrence woke the Barclay-Lloyds early, left The Gables and made his way down Pevensey Place. I don't expect I shall like her, he thought, Darius was probably exaggerating. But when he caught sight of her, lying in the sunshine on her front lawn, his heart leaped within his so much less bulky body.

'Hullo,' he said in a voice made gruff by embarrassment.

'Hullo,' she replied in a voice like honey, and she opened wide her amazing orange eyes.

'I haven't seen you around before,' she said. 'What's your name?'

'Lawrence,' muttered Lawrence.

'I'm Bella,' she said.

Bella, thought Lawrence. What a beautiful name! And what a beautiful cat! It's love at first sight! It's now or never!

'Bella,' he said. 'Could we be . . . friends?'

Bella stood up and stretched her elegant tortoiseshell-and-white body.

'Friends, yes, I dare say,' she replied. 'But nothing more.'

'Oh,' said Lawrence. 'You don't fancy me?'

'Frankly, Lawrence, no,' said Bella. 'I like the sound of you – you're nice, I'm sure – but you're much too slender for my taste, I've never cared for slim boys. I go for really well-covered types. As a matter of fact there's a black cat further up Pevensey Place – I haven't seen him about lately – but I really had a crush on him. Talk about fat, he was enormous! I do love a very, very fat cat, and he was the fattest!'

She sighed.

'If only I could meet him again one day,' she said.

You will! thought Lawrence. You will, and before very long too, and he padded away across the Park to be in time for breakfast at Rosevale, followed by lunch at Hillview, tea at Number 33, and then back for supper at The Gables, including a saucer of Gold Top and perhaps, if he could persuade the Barclay-Lloyds, second helpings. Oh, Bella, he thought as he hurried along. You just wait!

Illustrations by Mike Terry

Susan Gates

from Revenge of the Toffee Monster

Above their heads the cobwebs rustled. They were spiky with flies' legs and wings. Where did that cold gust of wind come from? It made the ribbons on Harold's cap flutter. Lenny looked nervously round. But there was no one in the tower room with them.

'Are you listening?' said Miss Butterworth sternly. He might be a guardian angel but he still needed telling. Even angels had to pay attention. And she was getting to the really important bit.

'One night,' said Miss Butterworth, her voice slow and dripping with doom, 'Josiah Butterworth created a living creature, made entirely out of brazil nut toffee.'

'Come on!' said Lenny. 'You're joking!' He meant to laugh: 'Ha, ha ha!' But somehow it came out as a nervous giggle.

'I *never* make jokes about toffee, young man!' declared Miss Butterworth, indignantly. She thought toffee was such marvellous stuff that it could be used for almost anything, including creating life. But even she had to admit, 'Well, Josiah *might* have added one or two secret ingredients.'

'You mean you're serious?' gasped Lenny. 'Where did he do it? Where did he create this living creature?'

'In this very room,' said Miss Butterworth, in a low and ghostly voice.

Lenny could feel the skin at the back of his neck crawl. He wriggled his shoulders to try and stop it.

'He was working late,' said Miss Butterworth. 'It was almost midnight. And there was a storm. They say it was the worst storm in living memory! Crashing thunder, great jagged forks of lightning. But Josiah didn't notice such things. He didn't even notice if it was day or night when he was busy with his frogs and his toffee and all his other experiments. On this particular night all his toffee machines were switched on. All humming away, flashing like traffic lights. This room was crackling with electricity! Massive voltages! Remember, people weren't used to electricity then – they didn't know how dangerous it could be. There was a huge copper vat of brazil nut toffee – over there!'

Miss Butterworth's arm flew out as she pointed into the darkness. Lenny's head whipped round. But there was nothing to see except trembling shadows.

'They say the vat was so big you could get a horse in it! Josiah never did things by halves! It had thick wires leading into it to heat up the toffee and to work a gigantic metal whisk that stirred it round and round. So it was humming along nicely, heating up and whisking . . . when things went terribly wrong. No one knew what really happened. All Josiah remembered was a hissing sound and thick black smoke and a smell like bonfires. Then he fell to the floor with his hair on end, stiff as a kipper. They think a great lightning bolt came through the glass roof. It struck the big copper vat of brazil nut toffee, a direct hit, and bingo, there was a gigantic bang – it was heard several streets away and the whole tower room lit up with blue flashes that could be seen right across the river!'

'This Toffee Creature –' said Lenny, in a quavering voice. He couldn't finish his sentence.

'Just wait! I'm coming to that! – So when my grandad Josiah Butterworth woke up, the vat was a smoking ruin. But out of it was climbing this creature, this living thing –'

'He must have nearly died of fright!' gasped Lenny. 'He must have wet himself!'

'He did not!' said Miss Butterworth. 'He was thrilled to bits! He jumped around with joy! He greeted the creature! He rushed to hug it but, of course, it was too sticky. 'My creation!' he cried. "My wonderful Toffee Creature!"'

'So did he make it deliberately then?' asked Lenny, his eyes boggling. 'Or was it an accident?'

'Who knows?' said Miss Butterworth, flinging her arms wide. 'Who knows what was in Josiah's mind? He was a toffee genius! He always knew, as I do, that toffee is a miraculous substance. That it has limitless possibilities! And when he was a boy his hero was Dr Frankenstein. But who knows? Whether he did it deliberately or not, his Toffee Creature was born.'

'Where was Harold when all this was going on?'

'He was asleep in bed in Butterworth Towers, just next door to the Toffee Works. Anyhow, Josiah was so excited by what he'd created that he went rushing to wake Harold up. He brought him back to this room to see the incredible creature.'

'Don't tell me Harold wasn't scared stiff!'

'He was at first. But remember, poor little Harold was a lonely and neglected boy. He had no friends. Even his mum and dad ignored him. So after a time, he and the Toffee Creature became constant companions. The creature followed him round like a dog –'

'What did it look like?' asked Lenny, more excited now than scared. 'I can't imagine what a Toffee Creature would look like!'

'It was very strange,' mused Miss Butterworth. 'Of course, I didn't see it myself. I only know about this from family stories. But they say it looked very lumpy and warty. You'd expect that, I suppose, because it was made of brazil nut toffee. In some ways it looked like a great grizzly bear – a bear made out of toffee, of course. But in other ways it looked very frog-like. It had rather goggly eyes and a big stretchy mouth and webbed feet and hands and these springy back legs –'

'Did it talk? What did it say?'

'It couldn't talk. You can't expect miracles! It was a very crude life form. They say it made some sort of croaking sound when it was upset. And it wasn't very brainy, poor thing. In fact, it was thick as two short planks. It could only be taught one command: "Fetch!" It loved fetching things for people. Slippers, pipes, Harold's little horse. Anything it thought they needed. It only wanted to be helpful. It wanted people to say "Good Toffee Creature" and pat it on the head. But of course they never did because everything it fetched was ruined.'

'Was that because it was all sticky?'

'That's right.' Miss Butterworth shook her head and sighed. 'It was a warm-blooded creature so obviously the toffee never really set properly. You couldn't pat it on the head, even if you'd wanted to, because your hand would have stuck. As a life form it was a total disaster. It caused commotion wherever it went. Of course it couldn't go far. It had to be hidden at Butterworth Towers. It couldn't be taken out in public. Imagine it looming up out of a London fog! There would have been mass panic! In the end, even keeping it in the house was impossible.'

Lenny imagined the sticky Toffee Creature lumbering around his own living-room, desperately trying to be helpful. It would drive his mum bananas! 'Put that down!' his mum would say. 'Don't touch those Babygros. You've got sticky finger-marks everywhere!' If the Toffee Creature tried to fetch you something, say your football magazine, you'd have to rip it off its hands like Velcro! And then it would be torn to shreds and the pages would all stick together. And what if it tried to pick up his new baby sister to stop her crying? Lenny cringed at the thought . . .

'I bet it was always getting told off,' said Lenny, glumly. 'I bet it was always in trouble!'

'It was,' agreed Miss Butterworth. 'It couldn't do anything right. The servants hated it because it made more work for them. They had to clean up wherever it went. Harold's mother called it a hideous creature. It was banished to the Toffee Works where it made a kind of nest in the burnt-out vat it was born in. Even its master, Josiah, lost interest in it when he found out it wasn't very bright. I think he was secretly hoping his creation would be a genius, like him.'

'That's terrible,' said Lenny. 'You seen those stickers in cars, "A dog is for life and not just for Christmas"? Josiah shouldn't have made it, should he, if he didn't want to look after it? I mean, a Toffee Creature is for life, isn't it, even if it does try to pick up your baby sister!'

Miss Butterworth looked utterly baffled at Lenny's outburst. But she went on. 'Not everyone hated the Toffee Creature. Not everyone insulted it and drove it away. Harold saw past the stickiness and the wartiness and the mess. He saw it was a gentle, timid creature who only wanted some kindness. He and Clum –'

'Clum?' interrupted Lenny. 'Who's Clum?'

'Ah,' said Miss Butterworth, 'I forgot to tell you. Everyone was always saying, "Go away, you clumsy creature!" and "How clumsy you are!" to the Toffee Creature. So naturally it thought its name was Clumsy. Harold didn't like that name – so he shortened it to Clum and –'

'My Granny Wang had a dog who thought its name was "Down boy!" Lenny burst in. 'So what happened then? Did Harold and Clum become best friends?'

'I was going to tell you,' said Miss Butterworth, 'before you rudely interrupted.'

'Sorry,' said Lenny, smacking a hand over his mouth to make himself shut up.

'Harold and Clum were a pair, like eggs and bacon, cheese and pickle. They were inseparable! Clum thought he was a Butterworth too. Harold used to lead him round the Toffee Works – not by the hand, of course, because they would have stuck together.'

Lenny's hand was still resting on Harold's broken toy horse. Almost without thinking, he stroked its wooden head. And suddenly an amazing picture flashed into his mind. Of Harold and Clum here in this very room. He could see them now. Harold, that chubby, serious child in his lacy frock and button-up boots, pulling his little toy horse. And shambling behind him, Clum the Toffee Creature, with his great, big froggy head and goggly eyes gazing adoringly at little Harold, his best and only friend.

Lenny forgot he'd promised not to interrupt. 'Where's the toffee vat Clum lived in?' he said looking around the tower room. He couldn't see it. Perhaps it was hidden away behind the massive humbug machine.

'I don't know,' said Miss Butterworth. 'It was taken away long ago.

Lenny looked disappointed. Harold's things were here, in the Butterworth's private museum. His clothes were here and his toys. But there was nothing here, nothing that he could look at or touch, that would make Clum seem as real to him as poor little Harold did.

'Isn't there anything left of Clum?'

'What do you mean?' demanded Miss Butterworth, flashing him a suspicious look. For a moment Lenny thought that she looked scared. But no, he must have been mistaken. Miss Butterworth was like a fierce, snappy little terrier. She wasn't afraid of anything.

'I mean, like a picture of him or something?' said Lenny. 'Anything to remind people of him?'

'Oh,' said Miss Butterworth, smiling her twisted smile. 'I see what you mean. No, there are no pictures.'

Lenny nodded sadly. Then a monstrous thought sprang into his brain. The shock of it made him shiver. It made him feel hot, then icy cold.

'Clum isn't . . . he isn't . . .' stammered Lenny, 'he isn't alive now, is he? He doesn't still live here, in the Toffee Works? I mean, how long do Toffee Creatures live?'

A scratching sound somewhere above him made his heart leap, his eyes fly upwards. But it was only a pigeon, scrabbling about on the glass dome.

'No,' said Miss Butterworth, choosing her words very carefully. 'He isn't *alive* here now. He perished over a hundred years ago, in the year 1887 to be precise –'

Lenny's breath came out in a long sigh. 'Phew! Thank goodness!'

'– on the night of young Master Harold's tragic accident.'

Miss Butterworth paused, sighed and adjusted her hair-net. It was tiring work bringing Lenny up to date on the Butterworths' family history. Her voice was fading to a whisper. She hadn't used it so much for a long, long time. This boy was from the strange and alien world outside the Toffee Works. But he had toffee in his blood, she was certain. And he'd been specially sent as Butterworth's guardian angel. That gave him the right to know. She decided to finish the job before her voice gave out altogether.

'That night,' she said, 'Harold's mother came to the Toffee Works from Butterworth Towers, a thing she never, ever did. But she had to give Josiah Butterworth an important message. She was all dressed up to go to the ball. She was at her most beautiful. She looked like a fairy princess! She sparkled with jewellery. She had a beautiful silver ballgown on that glittered in the light! Harold and Clum were bewitched by her! Of course, Harold knew he mustn't touch or hug his mother when she was dressed up in all her finery. But poor Clum didn't know that. He wanted to please her. He tried to fetch the fan that she'd left by the door and all the beautiful peacock feathers stuck to his hand. And then when he rushed to take it to her, his other hand touched her silver dress!'

'Oh no! Oh no!' gasped Lenny. 'I bet she went ballistic!'

'She screamed,' agreed Miss Butterworth. 'She had hysterics! She scared poor Clum out of the few wits he had. He hated people shouting and screaming. It really upset him. He was bewildered. He didn't know what he'd done wrong. She shrieked and shrieked at him: "You've ruined my gown, you clumsy, useless creature! Do you know how much that cost?" She took a make-up mirror out of her matching silver evening purse. She held it up. She said, "Look at yourself, you ugly creature! You are a beast, a monster! You should be in a cage, not allowed to mix with decent, civilized people! You are a freak of nature!" And Clum looked in the mirror and saw his own face.'

'And what did he do,' said Lenny in a hushed voice,

'when he found out he wasn't a Butterworth? That he wasn't even human? That he was all warty and looked like something out of a horror film?'

'They say he gave a great, heart-rending croak of anguish. He dashed the mirror to the ground. Then he hopped off to hide in the copper vat. Everyone was rushing around. Fanning Mrs Butterworth, giving her smelling salts. There was a real to-do! Only Harold went after the poor creature, to try and comfort him.'

Lenny looked round the gloomy tower room. He could imagine it happening. Clum rushing here to hide after he'd found out he was a freak. Little Harold hurrying after him –

'That day,' said Miss Butterworth in a voice grim as graveyards, 'the humbug machine was running full pelt – there was a big humbug order to fill. Harold came dashing in. He didn't think. He was only concerned for his friend. Before Clum could reach his vat, Harold threw himself at him to give him a big hug. It was the only time in his short life that the creature had ever been hugged. He was so overjoyed he put his arms round Harold. He lifted him high in the air –'

Lenny's hand flew up to his mouth. 'Oh no, I can't believe it! They stuck together, didn't they?'

'They did. And Harold panicked. He shouted, "Set me down!" But Clum didn't understand and only squeezed him tighter. Clum didn't know his own strength and poor Harold couldn't breathe. He struggled to get free from the creature's sticky embrace. But he fell –'

Lenny gnawed at his knuckles. It was too awful to

think about. 'Harold didn't fall into the humbug machine, did he? Is that what you meant when you said he came to a sticky end?' He looked fearfully at the great machine towering above them. He imagined those great iron paddles whacking the toffee mixture, spitting it out as humbugs, flicking it into tins. The thought of Harold being turned into humbugs was more than he could bear.

'Good heavens,' said Miss Butterworth. 'What gruesome minds you modern children have got! No, Harold didn't fall *into* the machine. He struck his head on one of the paddles as he fell. Clum saw Harold wasn't moving. He cried toffee tears. His poor heart was broken in two.'

'Where was Harold's dad all this time then? Where was Josiah?'

'He rushed in at that very moment with all his toffee workers behind him. They saw what had happened to poor Harold. They saw Clum crouching over him, croaking. And they began howling for revenge!'

'They didn't hurt Clum, did they?'

Miss Butterworth's voice was getting weaker, as she neared the tragic end of her tale.

'Clum slipped past them, out of the tower room, out of the Toffee Works and on to the streets. It was dark and no one could see him. It was winter; there was snow on the ground. More toffee workers joined the chase. They turned into a baying mob with torches and dogs. Clum was terrified and mad with grief. Once they nearly caught him. He turned on them. The poor hunted brute couldn't take any more. He stretched himself up to his full height. He was over seven feet tall! "Careful, he's dangerous!" someone called. So they loosed the dogs but he batted them away with his webbed hands and they ran off yelping into the dark. He got away. He half-hopped, half-ran until he came to the river. There was thick ice covering it, all the way across. He went out on to the ice. The mob wasn't far behind. He could see the blazing torches and hear the men chanting, "Kill the creature! Kill it!" For the first time in his life he was graceful, sliding on the ice, swooping across it like a bird. But in the middle he stopped. The mob crowded on to the river bank, waiting to see what he would do.'

Lenny's face was screwed up in horror. He almost covered up his ears. He didn't want to hear the next bit of the story. But Miss Butterworth went on, relentlessly. Her weary voice was no louder than the rustle of dry leaves. Lenny had to concentrate really hard to hear it.

'They say,' said Miss Butterworth, 'that he turned to look back at the screaming mob, just once. Then he looked up at the shining moon. He seemed to reach out for it, trying to fetch it. He loved silvery things, remember. Then he gave a last despairing croak and jumped up and down on the ice until it cracked beneath him. He let himself slip into the icy water.'

'He could have saved himself!' cried Lenny in anguish. 'He had webbed feet, didn't he? He could have swum!'

'Well, he didn't,' whispered Miss Butter-worth, shaking her head. 'He was carried away beneath the ice. The water that day was well below freezing. The mob raced along the bank after him. Further downstream Clum got tangled in some weed. They could see him under the ice. They smashed a hole in it to get to him. When they dragged him out it was far too late. The cold had killed him. He was frozen stiff as stone.'

Jim Eldridge

'Into Combat'

adapted from Warpath 7: Night Bomber

My chance to fly a combat mission with my new crewmates came the very next night. As I climbed on board the Lancaster, I couldn't help thinking about the last time I'd flown. Then I'd been smiling and joking with a different set of men. All of them gone now. This time I found it hard to put on a smiling face.

'Cheer up, John,' said Steve, with a grin. 'You can only die once.'

I forced a smile, but over his shoulder I could see Wally's face glaring at me and I knew that this was a make-or-break flight for me. If we crashed and I was the only survivor, I knew I'd never be able to set foot in another plane again.

We took our places and I strapped myself in. As flight engineer, I got to sit next to the pilot. The rest of the crew were in their own solitary stations. Bruce, our tail gunner, was in a turret at the rear of the plane. Steve, our mid-upper gunner, sat in a revolving turret right at the top of the plane. Our bomb aimer, Andrew, sat in the forward turret below me, and George, our radio operator, was stationed well behind my position. Wally, our navigator, was in his own little compartment, behind the pilot's seat. He was the only crew member allowed to have a light on, so that he could check his maps, and this meant his position was curtained off. As flight engineer I had to act as an assistant during take-off. Once we were in the air, I had to look after the distribution of fuel to the different engines and carry out repairs.

We went through the standard starting-up procedure, completing all the checks and then firing up the engines. All across the airfield, I could see other Lancasters going through the same process. Bob looked over to me, and I gave him the thumbs up. Everything seemed fine. We were ready to go.

Bob signalled to the ground crew and they removed the chocks that held our wheels in place. We rolled forward and joined the queue of Lancasters taxiing slowly towards the end of the runway. I watched as the plane ahead of us took to the skies. Then it was our turn.

We went through the last-minute checks and a green light from the control tower told us that we were clear for take-off. Releasing the brakes, Bob slowly opened the throttles. He eased forward on the control column and we quickly began to move forward. As the airspeed indicator registered 100 mph, he applied backward pressure on the column. Suddenly we were airborne!

Within seconds we were at 500 feet and travelling at 125 mph. We began our climb.

When we reached 16,000 feet our temperature dropped. The Lancaster may have been 25 tons of wonderful fighting machine, but it was also as cold and draughty as an igloo with holes in the walls. We were all kitted out with electrically heated suits, which in theory should have kept us warm, but in practice it didn't work that way. With the icy cold outside and the electrical circuits in the suits malfunctioning every so often, you stood a good chance of either getting burns from your suit overheating, or frostbite from it cutting out altogether.

We headed through the night sky towards our target, flying at 22,000 feet and at about 200 mph. It was almost three hours before we finally saw land.

'German coast five miles ahead,' Wally warned.

'Roger,' responded Bob.

So far, it had been a fairly quiet trip.

'Ten minutes to target,' Wally informed us.

'Fighter coming in from the rear!' Bruce's voice suddenly shouted.

I could hear the whine of tracer from the incoming fighter. We were in trouble.

'Coming in from starboard!' shouted Bruce.

Bob immediately turned the Lancaster to port, to miss the line of tracer from the German fighter. He began to weave the huge plane from side to side, desperately trying to avoid enemy fire.

Suddenly, there was an explosion on our starboard side that lit up the night sky.

'Got him!' roared Steve.

'Five minutes to target,' reported Wally.

'Taking up position at the bombsight,' Andrew replied.

As we approached, I could hear Andrew's voice guiding Bob towards the target.

'Right . . . steady . . . steady . . . left . . . right . . . right a bit more . . . OK.'

There was a loud click as Andrew released the bombs.

'Bombs gone!'

We all waited for the plane's usual surge upwards as the bomb load was dropped, making us that much lighter. But it didn't happen.

'What's up, Andrew?' called Bob. 'Something wrong?'

'The mechanism's jammed! The bombs are stuck in the hold!' he shouted.

As I heard Andrew's words, a hollow feeling crept into the pit of my stomach. It was me, the jinx, bringing them bad luck, just as I'd brought bad luck to my two previous crews.

'I'll check it, skipper,' I said.

'My job,' came Andrew's voice. 'I'll do it!'

'I'm the engineer,' I reminded him. 'If it's a faulty mechanism, I'll know what to do.'

I said it with more confidence than I felt. All I knew was that I had to get those bombs unloaded. If I didn't, their extra weight would mean we'd run out of fuel long before we got back to England. Ditching into the sea, with the weight of those bombs, would drown us all for sure.

I made my way down to the bomb bay and lifted the inspection covers above it. The doors were open, and far, far below, I could see the explosions as the other bombers hit the target. Our bombs were still securely stuck on their retaining hooks. I stretched my arms out to try to reach the hooks, but my fingers were just tantalisingly short.

'How you doing, John?' came Bob's voice in my earphones.

'Not good, skipper,' I reported. 'I'm going to have to chop away the floor to get to the hooks.'

'Better be quick about it,' said Bob. 'The flak's getting worse, and their fighters are starting to get a bearing on us.'

'We'll deal with them, skipper,' came Bruce's voice. 'Just get those bombs out of there, John.'

I took the fire-axe and began to chop away at the aluminium floor. I could hear the rattle of our machine guns as both Bruce and Steve opened fire, doing their best to keep the enemy at bay.

'Faster would be good, John,' said Bob urgently. 'I'll make one last pass over the target area, after that I'm going to have to turn and head for home, fully loaded.'

'Going as fast as I can, skipper!' I replied.

I heard someone approach behind me.

'Need any help, mate?' Andrew asked.

I nodded. 'I'm going to lean through the hole and smash the hooks off with the axe. Can you hold my legs while I do it?'

'Got it,' said Andrew, nodding.

I pushed myself forward through the hole until I was hanging over the open bomb bay. I felt Andrew get a hold of my legs and just hoped that his grip was tight. The ground was 20,000 feet below.

In this awkward position, I began hitting the hooks as hard as I could. My arms ached terribly as I hacked and hacked away.

'Careful! Don't hit the bombs!' warned Andrew.

I was too tired to even reply. I made one last exhausted swing and suddenly the hooks gave way. The bombs dropped, taking one of the doors with them. I lurched forward, and for a second I thought I was going to fall from the plane. Luckily, Andrew had a firm hold of my legs. I felt him grip them tightly. He pulled me back into the plane and I lay on the floor, panting.

'Bombs away, skipper!' I managed to gasp into my headset.

'Good job and on target,' said Bob with relief. 'Right, guys, we're heading home!'

Morris Gleitzman

from Gift of the Gab

1

It's not *fair.*

I don't reckon the police should lock people up without hearing their side of the story.

My side of the story's really simple.

I did it, but there was a reason.

I tried to explain to Sergeant Cleary why I did it. In the police car I wrote down in my notebook everything that happened today. Even the things that'll probably make Dad send me to bed early when he hears about them.

I showed my statement to Sergeant Cleary while he was locking me in this cell.

'Not now, Rowena,' he said.

I could see he wasn't interested, though that might have been because Dermot Figgis was trying to bite him.

Police officers in small country towns have it really tough. The police stations are always understaffed. The only other officer on duty here today is Constable Pola, but he has to stay at the front desk in case of emergency calls or exciting developments in the car racing on TV.

Once Sergeant Cleary got Dermot into a cell, I tried to explain again. I banged on a wall pipe with my pen, like they do in prison movies.

'Message from Rowena Batts,' I banged in Morse code. 'I only did it because of the dog poo.'

That was ten minutes ago.

Sergeant Cleary hasn't been back.

He probably doesn't know Morse code. Either that or I didn't send it properly because my hands are shaking so much from outrage at Dermot Figgis and from worry about what's going to happen to me.

Sergeant Cleary's probably ringing Dad now.

'Mr Batts?' he's probably saying. 'We've got Rowena in the lock-up. We'll be charging her and putting her on trial as a criminal.'

Just thinking about it gives me a lump in the guts bigger than Antarctica.

Poor Dad. I hate putting him through this. The shame. And the lawyer's fees. He's got enough on his plate with the root weevil in the back paddock.

If only the police would listen to me.

That's the worst thing about being born with bits missing from your throat and not being able to talk with your voice, some people just won't listen to you.

Which means they never hear your side of the story.

The police are hearing Dermot Figgis's side. They can't help hearing it, he's been yelling it from the next cell for the last fifteen minutes.

'Rowena Batts attacked my car,' he's yelling. 'She filled it up with stewed apples.'

He's right, I did, but as I said before, there was a reason.

It's all here in my notebook. Including diagrams so the jury at my trial can see exactly what happened.

Some of the diagrams are bit wobbly. It's hard to do neat drawing while your hands are trembling with outrage and indignation. The dog-poo diagram for example. It looks more like two shrivelled sausages. I'd better label it so there's no misunderstanding.

And I'd better draw a diagram of the war memorial so the jury can see where the whole thing started.

This morning at the Anzac Day dawn ceremony.

Anzac Day's a very special day for me and Dad. It's our most important day of the year, including Christmas, birthdays and the release of a new Carla Tamworth CD.

It's the day Mum died.

So if anyone spoils it, I get pretty ropable.

I started getting ropable with Dermot Figgis at about 6.05 this morning.

As the first rays of the sun appeared over the supermarket, the crowd around the war memorial went quiet and Mr Shapiro played 'The Last Post' on his trumpet. Then we started the two-minute silence for the Aussie soldiers and other people who died in wars.

Dad reckons there were millions of them, including his grandfather who died in World War One, so even though it's not the most important part of the day for me, I try to concentrate.

This morning it was impossible.

Dermot Figgis and some of his hoon mates were doing the sausages. The footy club always does a sausage sizzle on Anzac Day so people who get emotionally drained by the ceremony can have a hot breakfast after.

As the two-minute silence began, Dermot started chopping onions really loudly.

Everyone glared at him, including me.

Then I glanced anxiously at old Mr Wetherby. He was actually in World War One and saw quite a few of his mates die. It can really stress you if you're trying to think about people who've died and other people are chopping onions noisily, specially if you're ninety-eight.

I could see Mr Wetherby trembling in his wheelchair. For a sec I thought he was so angry he was having a seizure. Then I realised he was just excited because he was being filmed by a TV crew as one of the oldest diggers in the state.

Dermot carried on chopping.

I decided if I go that selfish and dopey when I'm eighteen, I'll book myself in for a brain transplant.

I should have given Dermot a brain transplant there and then.

I would have done if I'd known what he was going to do half an hour later.

The two-minute silence ended and Dad stepped forward and cleared his throat.

Everyone stared. Some people looked cross and others rolled their eyes.

'Oh no,' someone muttered.

I couldn't believe it. What were they upset about? They all knew Dad was going to sing, he does every year.

It couldn't have been his clothes. Me and Dad got up extra early this morning and put a lot of effort into choosing him a respectful Anzac Day outfit. Black boots. Black jeans. Black shirt except for a tiny bit of yellow fringing. And he'd swapped his cow-skull belt buckle for one with an angel riding a really clean Harley.

The TV cameraman swung his camera away from Mr Wetherby and pointed it at Dad. I don't think he'd seen an apple farmer that well-dressed before.

Mr Cosgrove, the president of the Anzac Day committee, was glaring at Dad even harder than he'd been glaring at Dermot Figgis.

'Excuse me,' I said to Mr Cosgrove sternly. 'I think you're forgetting something. Anzac Day isn't just the day we remember the victims of war, it's also the day my mother died.'

Mr Cosgrove didn't understand all the words, of course, because he doesn't speak sign language, but I could tell he got the gist because he gave a big sigh.

Dad sang the song he always sings at the Anzac Day dawn ceremony. It's a beautiful Carla Tamworth country and western ballad about a truck driver whose wife dies and for the rest of his life he refuses to sell his truck because it's got the impression of her bottom in the passenger seat.

It makes me very sad, that song, because Mum died soon after I was born, so I haven't got those sorts of lasting memories of her.

It affected everyone else too, even though Dad's not that great a singer. Mr Wetherby dabbed away a tear and quite a few other people put their heads in their hands.

I could tell everyone was having strong feelings.

All except Dermot Figgis.

I heard giggling and turned and there was Dermot, dopey blond dreadlocks jiggling as he and his mates pointed at Dad and stuffed hotdog buns in their mouths to stop themselves laughing.

They weren't doing a very good job.

World War One exploded in my head.

I stormed over to Dermot, determined to shut him up.

On the way I picked up a large plastic bottle of mustard.

2

The human brain's a weird thing.

When it's scared it stops working.

Mine did just now, when I heard Sergeant Cleary coming along the corridor towards the cells.

He's here to charge me, I thought, and transfer me to a remand centre for juvenile offenders.

Then my brain switched itself off.

I know why it did that. I spent five years in a special school once because of my throat problems and I never want to go back to an institution again. Not even if

I end up a top surgeon or private detective. I won't charge kids from institutions who need treatment or a missing pet or parent found, but I won't be able to go to them, they'll have to come and see me on my yacht.

It's OK, but. Sergeant Cleary didn't charge me. Not yet. He just came down to tell Dermot Figgis to be quiet.

Dermot's brain went into hibernation too when he saw me storming towards him this morning holding a large bottle of mustard.

The whole town knows I stuffed a live frog into a kid's mouth once, a kid who wasn't respectful to Mum's memory, and Dermot must have thought I was planning to squeeze a bottleful of mustard into his.

I wasn't. I was just going to threaten him with it, that's all.

Dermot stepped away uncertainly, trod on a raw sausage, slipped, fell backwards and ended up sitting in a plastic bin full of ice and water and drink cans.

His mates cacked themselves.

Dermot's face went dark red.

That's when I did a dumb thing. I put my hand out to help him up.

When I think about it now, I feel faint. Dermot's years older than me and he could have crushed my hand like sausage meat in that big paw of his.

He didn't, but.

He let me pull him up. Then, as his mates went silent and embarrassed, he realised what he'd done and snatched his hand away.

He glared down at me with narrow eyes.

'You're history, kid,' he growled.

'Cheese-brain,' I replied. He doesn't speak sign, but I could tell he got the gist because his face went an even darker red.

Shaking, I went back over to Dad and concentrated on listening to the last few verses of the song.

When Dad finished, rather than let any more hoons spoil our sad mood further, we hopped onto the tractor and went over to the cemetery.

Or we would have done if the tractor hadn't broken down halfway there.

'Poop,' said Dad, using his mouth, which he always does when he's cross with himself.

I knew Dad was wishing we'd brought the truck. The only reason we brought the tractor was because it was hooked up to a trailer-load of mouldy apples Dad had promised Mr Lorenzini for his pigs.

It wasn't so bad. We had the tractor going in under an hour. It would have been less, but the apples attracted a lot of flies so we could only work one-handed.

The tractor broke down again halfway into the cemetery carpark.

'You go on ahead, Tonto,' said Dad. 'I'll fix this mongrel and catch you up.'

I was really pleased to hear him say that, partly because I really wanted to get to Mum's grave, and partly because I could tell he wasn't angry.

Tonto was a character in his favourite TV show when he was a kid, and he never calls me it when he's angry.

That's an example of why my dad's so special. A lot of dads, if the tractor was being a real mongrel, would get totally and completely ropable and spoil the most special day of the year.

Not my dad.

No, it's me who ended up doing that.

I knew there was something wrong with Mum's grave even before I got close to it.

It's in the top part of the cemetery with a really good view over the town. Because it's on a slope, you can see the flat grassy part of the grave as well as the headstone when you climb up to it.

I saw two small black things on the grassy part.

I knew they weren't lizards because they didn't scuttle off as I crunched towards them through the dry grass.

When I saw what they were, I felt a stab in the guts.

Dog poo.

Some mangy mongrel had done a poo on my most special place in the world.

Luckily, I always carry tissues on Anzac Day. I pulled a handful from my pocket, grabbed the two long hard shrivelled black objects and chucked them as hard as I could into the bush at the back of the graveyard.

'Sorry, Mum,' I whispered.

Then I heard Dad crunching towards me, so I stuffed the tissues back into my pocket.

He didn't have to know.

No point making him suffer too.

Funny, me thinking that. Given what's happened since. Dad wouldn't have suffered half as much from a bit of dog poo as he will when he finds out what I've done.

Oh well, at least we had our special time with Mum today.

'You OK, Tonto?' said Dad after we'd sat by the grave for about half an hour, alone with our feelings.

'I'm fine,' I replied. 'What about you?'

Dad's been a bit depressed lately. He always gets a bit depressed around Mum's anniversary. This year he's been more down than usual. I reckon it's the root weevil in the back paddock.

'I'm fine too,' said Dad. 'Now we've had our special time.'

That's the great thing about a dad who can speak with his hands. You can have a conversation even when both your throats are clogged up with tears.

We stood up and gave each other the hug Mum would have given us if she'd been around.

That's when I heard it.

A horrible, braying, jeering sound coming from the trees at the top of the cemetery.

Dermot Figgis and his hoon mates.

They swaggered out into the open, yelling and pointing to us and laughing.

I realised what the braying sound was.

Dermot was singing Mum's special song. The one Dad had sung at the war memorial. OK, Dermot could do the tune a bit better than Dad, but he was doing it in a mocking, sneering voice.

My guts knotted.

Then suddenly I knew.

The dog poo.

Suddenly I knew how it had got onto Mum's grave.

A dog didn't leave it there.

A mongrel did.

I stared at Dermot and World War One and World War Two both exploded in my head at the same time.

Dad put a hand on my arm.

'Ignore him,' he muttered. 'He'll get his.'

Dad was right about that.

A couple of lines into the song, Dermot forgot the words, which Dad would never do. Dermot gave us the finger and ran laughing into the trees with the other hoons.

I don't remember Dad leading me back to the carpark.

All I remember is what I saw there behind some bushes up the other end of the carpark from the tractor.

My heart started thumping so hard I thought my special black Anzac Day T-shirt was going to rip.

Dermot Figgis's car.

I knew it was his because he's the only person in town with a 1983 Falcon sprayed purple.

Dad hadn't seen it. He was too busy frowning at the tractor.

'I don't reckon she'll make it to Lorenzini's place hauling all these apples,' said Dad, unhooking the trailer. 'The distributor's gunna cark it any sec. How do you feel about staying here with the trailer while I go and ask Mr Lorenzini to come and fetch you and the apples?'

I found myself nodding really hard.

'If those hoons come back, just ignore 'em,' said Dad. 'They're all whistle and wind.'

I pretended not to hear him.

Dad gave me a squeeze and chugged off on the tractor.

As soon as he was out of sight, I dragged the trailer up to the other end of the carpark. It took ages and I nearly dislocated my shoulder, but I did it.

Then I grabbed the spade off the back of the trailer, opened Dermot's driver's door and started shovelling gunky apples into his car as fast as I could.

It was hot work, but I got them all in. When I'd finished, the cow-pattern seat covers were buried and you couldn't see much of the steering wheel.

Then I had an extra idea. I groped down into the squishy apples till I felt Dermot's keys in the ignition. I started the engine, groped some more till I found the heater knob, switched the heater on full and locked all the doors.

Revenge felt good.

But only for a sec.

Dermot's angry yell, ringing out across the carpark, put an end to that.

Jeremy Strong

from The Hundred-Mile-An-Hour-Dog

1

Streaker is a mixed-up kind of dog. You can see from her thin body and powerful legs that she's got a lot of greyhound blood in her, along with quite a bit of Ferrari and a large chunk of whirlwind.

Nobody in our family likes walking her and this is hardly surprising. Streaker can out-accelerate a torpedo. She can do 0 to 100 mph in the blink of an eye. She's usually vanished over the far horizon long before you have time to yell – 'Streaker!'

Dad refuses to walk her, point-blank. 'I've got backache,' is his usual excuse, though how this stops him from walking I really haven't a clue.

I tried something similar once myself. 'I've got front-ache,' I said. Mum gave me a chilly glare and handed me the dog-lead. She'll do anything to get out of walking Streaker too, and that is how the whole thing started. I ended up having the craziest Easter holiday you can imagine.

'Trevor . . .' said Mum one morning at the beginning of the holiday, and she gave me one of her really big, innocent smiles. 'Trevor . . .' (I should have guessed she was up to something.) 'Trevor – I'll give you thirty pounds if you walk Streaker every day this holiday.'

Thirty pounds! As you can imagine, my eyes boggled a bit. I just about had to shove them back in their sockets. I was so astonished I never twigged that what my mother was actually suggesting was MAJOR BRIBERY.

'It's the Easter holiday,' she continued, climbing on to her exercise-bike and pulling a pink sweat band round her forehead. 'You've nothing better to do.'

'Thirty pounds?' I repeated. 'Walk her every day for two weeks?' Mum nodded and began to pedal. I sat down to have a think. Thirty pounds was a lot of money. I could do loads of things with that.

On the other hand – and this was the big crunch – I would have to walk Streaker.

Now, if someone came up to you in the street and said, 'Hey! What's the worst torture you can think of?', you might suggest boiling in oil, or having to watch golf on TV with your dad, or even the nine times table – which is one of my own personal nightmares. But without doubt I would have to say – walking Streaker. This was going to be a big decision for me.

I reckoned there had to be some way of controlling Streaker. After all, she was only a dog. Humans are cleverer than animals. Humans have bigger brains. Humans rule the animal kingdom.

I seem to remember that just as I was thinking this, Streaker came hurtling in from the kitchen and landed on my lap like a mini-meteorite. We both crashed to the floor, where she sat on my chest looking very pleased with herself.

Mum carried on quietly pedalling all this time. She must have known I'd give in. 'I'll do it,' I said. Mum gave a strange squeak and one of her feet slipped off a pedal. For some reason she looked even more pleased with herself than Streaker did.

'Can I have some money now?' I asked. (See? I'm not stupid.)

'Of course not.' (Mum's not stupid either.)

'How about half now and half when I finish?'

Mum free-wheeled. 'At the end of the holiday, when the job is finished, I'll give you the money.' So that was that. I had agreed to walk the dog every day for two weeks, and that turned out to be only one of my problems that Easter. I must have been totally mad.

2

I watched this film about a tank battle once. There were all these invincible armour-plated tanks. They were even bazooka-proof. The heroes were losing (of course), until Colonel Clever-clogs (I forget his real name) came up with his BRILLIANT PLAN. 'We must use the tank's own strength against itself,' he said. 'If it's impossible for a shell to get through all that armour plate, it must be impossible for a shell to get out. We shall blow them up from the inside.'

And that's exactly what they did – brilliant film! Dad didn't like it of course. He doesn't like noisy action films with lots of explosions. He prefers watching golf, but have you *ever* seen an exciting golf match? I reckon golf would be a lot more fun if there were a couple of tanks playing and a few explosions. It would be quite interesting to see a nice big tank rumble across the green, square up on the tee, lift its powerful barrel and shoot golf balls right across the golf-course.

So, what has all this got to do with Streaker? Well, I spent ages trying to work out the best way of dealing with the dog. I asked myself: what does Streaker do best?

There were several answers to this:

1. Make a pig of herself.
2. Dig huge holes in the lawn.
3. Smell.

But I reckoned that the one thing she really shone at was speed. Streaker was a rocket on four legs. Maybe I could use her fantastic speed to my own ends. And that was when I remembered my roller-skates.

I hadn't used them for months. (I hadn't seen them for months.) All I had to do was hang on to Streaker's lead and that way she would get exercised and I'd get a free ride. You've got to admit it was a pretty jammy idea. Mum and Dad didn't think much of it though.

Mum sat at the lunch table in silence, eating her 99 per cent fat-free yoghurt that tasted like washing-up water. She obviously wasn't impressed. (She didn't think much of the yoghurt either.)

'I know your clever ideas, Trevor,' said Dad. 'They never work.'

'Yes they do,' I protested.

'Look what happened when you tried to build an assault course in your bedroom.'

Parents have this amazing way of bringing your most spectacular failures into general conversation, don't they? I could feel myself turning bright red.

'That wasn't my fault. I didn't know that fixing a squiddly bit of rope to the ceiling would bring all the plaster down.' Dad grunted and Mum pushed the remains of her yoghurt across the table.

'Would you like to finish it for me?' she asked.

'Why do you keep trying to poison me?' I wanted to know. Mum gave me a wan smile and chewed the end of a celery stick.

I was determined to prove them wrong. I launched a major expeditionary search into the bowels of my wardrobe and eventually managed to find both rollerskates. I spun the wheels and they gave off a very satisfying *whssssssh.* How could this plan fail?

I kept Streaker tied to the gatepost while I put on my skates. Then I carefully unwound the lead from the gate, wrapped it round one wrist and crouched low behind her. 'OK, Streaker – lift-off!'

She hardly needed any encouragement. Her front paws churned away just like they do in cartoons and we were off, with Streaker's ears streaming out behind her like jet-trails. I was amazed by her strength and speed. Even pulling me didn't prevent her from quickly reaching something that felt like Mach one. Her legs pounded the pavement and she barked happily as we flew along. She loved it. I simply held on to the lead and felt the wind racing through my hair.

We skidded round the corner in great style and Streaker headed up the main road towards the street market. I reckoned it was time to slow down a bit, but of course I didn't have any brakes, and neither did the dog. Anyhow, by this time Streaker had switched to turbo-boost and there was no stopping her.

We hit the market at maximum speed, scattering shoppers in every direction. I held on for dear life as we zigzagged through the startled crowd, careering wildly from one side to the other. It was all I could do to stay upright.

Streaker suddenly swerved violently to one side to avoid a mesmerized old lady. I had to fling out one arm as a counter-balance and somehow I managed to get her handbag stuck on it.

'Help! I've been robbed! Stop that boy! He's taken my bag!'

In no time at all the whole market seemed to be after me, but there was no way I could stop and explain. Streaker was really enjoying herself. There's nothing she likes more than a good chase. She doesn't even care if she's chasing or being chased. We went screaming round corners so fast that my skates started to smoke. We lurched into stalls, sending them tumbling over and spilling their contents every which way, crashed into people and bounced off them, and all the time the crowd behind was getting bigger and bigger and noisier and noisier.

'Stop that boy!'

'He's stolen an old bag's lady – I mean an old lady's bag!'

'Get the bag-snatcher!'

Streaker whizzed round the next corner so fast that she rolled over and over, and of course I just carried straight on and smashed headlong into a rack of dresses. Before I knew it I was hauled to my feet by a very angry mob. Not only was I still clutching the old lady's handbag, but I had a rather stunning flower-print sun-dress draped fetchingly over one shoulder

To cut a long story short, I was carted off to the police station, along with Streaker. She sat attentively in the corner and looked completely innocent while I was almost arrested. Just to make matters worse, the policeman on desk-duty was Sergeant Smugg. He lives just up the road from us and he's got three Alsatians. (Personally speaking, I think half an Alsatian is a bit too much, but three!)

Sergeant Smugg rang home and Dad had to come and get us. He wasn't very pleased, and not just because he had been dragged away from a nice kip on the sofa. Dad caught Sergeant Smugg cheating in a golf match last summer and they have been at war with each other ever since.

I explained that it was all an accident. It was Streaker's fault.

Sergeant Smugg looked at the ceiling and rolled his

eyes. 'Of course,' he said heavily. 'I should have known. The dog did it. The dog stole the handbag.'

'That isn't what I meant,' I said, and I tried to explain about the roller-skates and being towed and everything. Sergeant Smugg started laughing silently – you know, a sort of 'ha ha ha do you really expect me to believe that!' kind of laugh.

Dad was getting more and more annoyed at having his time wasted. 'It's quite obvious that Trevor is telling the truth, Mr Smugg,' he snapped. 'He's hardly likely to make up such a story. It was the dog's fault. She's like it all the time.'

The policeman looked across at Streaker, who was still sitting there angelically. '*Sergeant* Smugg, if you don't mind, not Mister,' he insisted. 'And you can hardly blame the poor dog for all this.'

At that point the 'poor dog' suddenly came to life. Streaker leaped up, raced across the room, launched herself across the sergeant's desk (scattering everything on it to the four winds) and threw herself cheerfully into Dad's lap, despite the fact that he was standing up. They both fell in a heap on the floor and Streaker proceeded to give Dad's ears a good clean-out.

'What did she do that for?' demanded Sergeant Smugg.

'No idea at all,' Dad answered from floor-level. 'I told you – she's like this all the time.'

Sergeant Smugg frowned and shook his head. 'Your dog's loopy. She needs to see a dog-psychiatrist.' And he let us go home.

I won't bore you with all the things Dad said on the

way back, but most of them carried threats of instant death. So, my first plan had proved spectacularly unsuccessful. Maybe it was time to call in reinforcements. I decided to go and see my best friend, Tina.

Illustrations by Nick Sharratt

Illustrations by Martin Chatterton

£1* *off any Puffin book*

Take this voucher along to any bookstore in the UK and Ireland. This voucher is valid until December 31st 2000 and only valid for the purchase of a PUFFIN BOOK.

* **Conditions:** Defaced or photocopied vouchers will not be accepted. Only one voucher per purchase. This voucher can only be redeemed against any **PUFFIN BOOK** sold at the recommended retail price and cannot be used in conjunction with any other price promotion or product. Offer applies only to items in stock at the time of your visit. Offer closes 31/12/00. The full address of Penguin Books Ltd. (promoter) can be found on the copyright/imprint page of this book. Cash redemption value: 0.0001p

£1* *off any Puffin book*

Take this voucher along to any bookstore in the UK and Ireland. This voucher is valid until December 31st 2000 and only valid for the purchase of a PUFFIN BOOK.

* **Conditions:** Defaced or photocopied vouchers will not be accepted. Only one voucher per purchase. This voucher can only be redeemed against any **PUFFIN BOOK** sold at the recommended retail price and cannot be used in conjunction with any other price promotion or product. Offer applies only to items in stock at the time of your visit. Offer closes 31/12/00. The full address of Penguin Books Ltd. (promoter) can be found on the copyright/imprint page of this book. Cash redemption value: 0.0001p

Dear Bookseller

Please ensure that you only accept this voucher in accordance with the terms overleaf. Then return this voucher before 31 January 2001 to:

Puffin Books Go For It! Offer, PCS Marketing & Computing Ltd. 80 Buckingham Avenue, Slough, Berkshire SL1 4PN

Puffin Books will ensure, on presentation of this voucher, that you are refunded, or your account will be credited (if you have an account with us), £1 for one PUFFIN BOOK sold before 31 December 2000.

To be completed by the bookseller:

BOOKSHOP ....

ADDRESS ....

....

....

POSTCODE ....

DATE ....

PENGUIN ACCOUNT NO. ....

(if known)

Proof of posting will not be accepted as proof of delivery cash value 0.0001p

Dear Bookseller

Please ensure that you only accept this voucher in accordance with the terms overleaf. Then return this voucher before 31 January 2001 to:

Puffin Books Go For It! Offer, PCS Marketing & Computing Ltd. 80 Buckingham Avenue, Slough, Berkshire SL1 4PN

Puffin Books will ensure, on presentation of this voucher, that you are refunded, or your account will be credited (if you have an account with us), £1 for one PUFFIN BOOK sold before 31 December 2000.

To be completed by the bookseller:

BOOKSHOP ....

ADDRESS ....

....

....

POSTCODE ....

DATE ....

PENGUIN ACCOUNT NO. ....

(if known)

Proof of posting will not be accepted as proof of delivery cash value 0.0001p

Dear Bookseller

Please ensure that you only accept this voucher in accordance with the terms overleaf. Then return this voucher before 31 January 2001 to:

Puffin Books Go For It! Offer, PCS Marketing & Computing Ltd. 80 Buckingham Avenue, Slough, Berkshire SL1 4PN

Puffin Books will ensure, on presentation of this voucher, that you are refunded, or your account will be credited (if you have an account with us), £1 for one PUFFIN BOOK sold before 31 December 2000.

To be completed by the bookseller:

BOOKSHOP ....

ADDRESS ....

....

....

POSTCODE ....

DATE ....

PENGUIN ACCOUNT NO. ....

(if known)

Proof of posting will not be accepted as proof of delivery cash value 0.0001p

£1* *off any Puffin book*

Take this voucher along to any bookstore in the UK and Ireland. This voucher is valid until December 31st 2000 and only valid for the purchase of a PUFFIN BOOK.

* **Conditions:** Defaced or photocopied vouchers will not be accepted. Only one voucher per purchase. This voucher can only be redeemed against any **PUFFIN BOOK** sold at the recommended retail price and cannot be used in conjunction with any other price promotion or product. Offer applies only to items in stock at the time of your visit. Offer closes 31/12/00. The full address of Penguin Books Ltd. (promoter) can be found on the copyright/imprint page of this book. Cash redemption value: 0.0001p

£1* *off any Puffin book*

Take this voucher along to any bookstore in the UK and Ireland. This voucher is valid until December 31st 2000 and only valid for the purchase of a PUFFIN BOOK.

* **Conditions:** Defaced or photocopied vouchers will not be accepted. Only one voucher per purchase. This voucher can only be redeemed against any **PUFFIN BOOK** sold at the recommended retail price and cannot be used in conjunction with any other price promotion or product. Offer applies only to items in stock at the time of your visit. Offer closes 31/12/00. The full address of Penguin Books Ltd. (promoter) can be found on the copyright/imprint page of this book. Cash redemption value: 0.0001p

£1* *off any Puffin book*

Take this voucher along to any bookstore in the UK and Ireland. This voucher is valid until December 31st 2000 and only valid for the purchase of a PUFFIN BOOK.

* **Conditions:** Defaced or photocopied vouchers will not be accepted. Only one voucher per purchase. This voucher can only be redeemed against any **PUFFIN BOOK** sold at the recommended retail price and cannot be used in conjunction with any other price promotion or product. Offer applies only to items in stock at the time of your visit. Offer closes 31/12/00. The full address of Penguin Books Ltd. (promoter) can be found on the copyright/imprint page of this book. Cash redemption value: 0.0001p

Dear Bookseller

Please ensure that you only accept this voucher in accordance with the terms overleaf. Then return this voucher before 31 January 2001 to:

Puffin Books Go For It! Offer, PCS Marketing & Computing Ltd. 80 Buckingham Avenue, Slough, Berkshire SL1 4PN

Puffin Books will ensure, on presentation of this voucher, that you are refunded, or your account will be credited (if you have an account with us), £1 for one PUFFIN BOOK sold before 31 December 2000.

To be completed by the bookseller:

BOOKSHOP ....

ADDRESS ....

....

....

POSTCODE ....

DATE ....

PENGUIN ACCOUNT NO. ....

(if known)

Proof of posting will not be accepted as proof of delivery cash value 0.0001p

Dear Bookseller

Please ensure that you only accept this voucher in accordance with the terms overleaf. Then return this voucher before 31 January 2001 to:

Puffin Books Go For It! Offer, PCS Marketing & Computing Ltd. 80 Buckingham Avenue, Slough, Berkshire SL1 4PN

Puffin Books will ensure, on presentation of this voucher, that you are refunded, or your account will be credited (if you have an account with us), £1 for one PUFFIN BOOK sold before 31 December 2000.

To be completed by the bookseller:

BOOKSHOP ....

ADDRESS ....

....

....

POSTCODE ....

DATE ....

PENGUIN ACCOUNT NO. ....

(if known)

Proof of posting will not be accepted as proof of delivery cash value 0.0001p

Dear Bookseller

Please ensure that you only accept this voucher in accordance with the terms overleaf. Then return this voucher before 31 January 2001 to:

Puffin Books Go For It! Offer, PCS Marketing & Computing Ltd. 80 Buckingham Avenue, Slough, Berkshire SL1 4PN

Puffin Books will ensure, on presentation of this voucher, that you are refunded, or your account will be credited (if you have an account with us), £1 for one PUFFIN BOOK sold before 31 December 2000.

To be completed by the bookseller:

BOOKSHOP ....

ADDRESS ....

....

....

POSTCODE ....

DATE ....

PENGUIN ACCOUNT NO. ....

(if known)

Proof of posting will not be accepted as proof of delivery cash value 0.0001p

Acknowledgements

The editor and publishers gratefully acknowledge the following for permission to reproduce copyright stories in this book:

The Hooligan's Shampoo by Philip Ridley, first published by Puffin Books, 1996, copyright © Philip Ridley, 1996; Extract from *MacB* by Neil Arksey, first published by Puffin Books, 1999, copyright © Neil Arksey, 1999; Extract from *The Demon Headmaster* by Gillian Cross, first published by Oxford University Press, 1982, copyright © Gillian Cross, 1982; 'Fight the Good Fight' from *Keep It in the Family* by Anne Fine, published by Penguin Books, 1996, first published in *Streets Ahead* (Ed. Valerie Bierman) by Methuen Children's Books, 1989, copyright © Anne Fine, 1989; Extract from *Matilda* by Roald Dahl, published in Puffin Books 1989, first published by Jonathan Cape Ltd, 1988, copyright © Roald Dahl Nominee Ltd, 1988; *The Spitting Rat* by Paul Jennings, first published by Penguin Books Australia, 1999, copyright © Greenleaves Pty Ltd, 1999; Extract from *Survive! Volcanic Fury* by Jack Dillon, first published by Puffin Books, 1999, copyright © Working Partners Ltd, 1999; 'Fat Lawrence' from *Animal Stories* by Dick King-Smith, first published by Viking, 1997, copyright © Fox Busters Ltd, 1997; Extract from *Revenge of the Toffee Monster* by Susan Gates, first published by Puffin Books, 1999, copyright © Susan Gates, 1999; Extract from *Warpath 7: Night Bomber* by J. Eldrdige, first published by Puffin Books, 1999, copyright © J. Eldridge, 1999; Extract from *Gift of the Gab* by Morris Gleitzman, first published by Penguin Books Australia, 1999, copyright © Creative Input Pty Ltd, 1999; Extract from *The Hundred-Mile-An-Hour Dog* by Jeremy Strong, first published by Viking, 1996, copyright © Jeremy Strong, 1996